The Prince's Vessel

S. Rodman

Dark Angst Publishing

Copyright © 2023 by S. Rodman

All rights reserved.

No portion of this book may be reproduced in any form without written permission from the publisher or author, except as permitted by U.S. copyright law.

ISBN: 9798851994289

Cover design by Miblart.

ALL RIGHTS RESERVED: This literary work may not be reproduced or transmitted in any form or by any means, including electronic or photographic reproduction, in whole or in part, without express written permission.

All characters and events in this book are fictitious. Any resemblance to actual persons living or dead is strictly coincidental.

WARNING: The unauthorized reproduction or distribution of this copyrighted work is illegal. Criminal copyright infringement, including infringement without monetary gain, is investigated by the FBI and is punishable by up to 5 years in federal prison and a fine of $250,000.

This book contains,

Reference to, and a paragraph long flashback of, a SA a main character endured when he was a teenager.

On page depiction of near dubious consent between a main character and a side character, before the MC is rescued by the other MC.

A villain uses the threat of inflicting SA on a side character as a means of trying to control a MC.

On page murder

Contents

1. Chapter 1 — 1
2. Chapter 2 — 5
3. Chapter 3 — 19
4. Chapter 4 — 23
5. Chapter 5 — 31
6. Chapter 6 — 37
7. Chapter 7 — 43
8. Chapter 8 — 49
9. Chapter 9 — 55
10. Chapter 10 — 59
11. Chapter 11 — 65
12. Chapter 12 — 71
13. Chapter 13 — 77
14. Chapter 14 — 83

15.	Chapter 15	89
16.	Chapter 16	95
17.	Chapter 17	101
18.	Chapter 18	107
19.	Chapter 19	113
20.	Chapter 20	117
21.	Chapter 21	123
22.	Chapter 22	129
23.	Chapter 23	135
24.	Chapter 24	141
25.	Chapter 25	147
26.	Chapter 26	151
27.	Chapter 27	157
28.	Chapter 28	161
29.	Chapter 29	167
30.	Chapter 30	175
31.	Chapter 31	181
Coming Soon		187
Thank You		189
Books By S. Rodman		191

Chapter One

Jem

'You have the honor of entertaining Prince Wilhelm of Bavaria. A car will pick you up at seven p.m.'

It's so tempting to throw my phone across the room and smash it against the wall. But if I do that, I'm just playing along with the temperamental vessel stereotype. So, I'm going to take a deep breath and calm down instead. I will not throw a strop over a text message.

It's all fine anyway. It's just condescending words, it means nothing. Someone needs to empty me today and it might as well be a visiting prince. I get to do my diplomatic duty, while having my needs met. It's all good.

Implying that I should be honored to take the cock of a prince is galling, but heaven knows I've had far worse insults in my life. And besides, I've never had a prince before. It will just be another old man grunting on top of me, but I can count it as a new notch for my bedpost.

The door to the drawing room flings open and Colby bounces in like an overexcited puppy. He bounds right up to me and shoves a tablet under my nose.

"Look!" he exclaims.

I cast my eyes over a montage of photos of women.

"What am I looking at?" I ask.

"Surrogates!" squeals Colby.

I feel my eyebrows rise in disdain. Surrogates? Colby hasn't been married to my brother for long at all. And he is only in his early twenties. Why the rush to parenthood? But I suppose my brother does need an heir and a spare. Someone to pass the Duke Sothbridge title to.

I sigh in resignation. It's not like parenting is hard work for Old Blood. Dust off the nursery in the south wing, hire an army of nannies. Send the little darlings off to boarding school when they are a little older.

"Congratulations," I say weakly.

Colby beams at me, and I instantly feel bad. He is a sweetie. A complete ball of sunshine. As well as sickeningly loved up with my brother, despite their rocky start.

Colby will probably be a great parent and far more hands on than mine and Harry's ever were. He deserves the benefit of doubt at the very least. I can give him that much.

"You are going to be an amazing uncle! The baby will be so lucky to have you, another adult who will always be here."

He is smiling and his eyes are glowing with happiness, but his words cut into me like knives. The easy assumption that I will always be here. Living in the house I was born in. A mere addition to my brother's household. Even if I outlive him, I will still linger here. A family member inherited along with the title. Beholden to my as yet unborn nephew.

It's an incredibly depressing thought. All the more horrid for its accuracy. The long, lonely years of my life are going to stretch out just like that. I'll live here, be sent to various mages to be emptied of magic until I'm middle-aged and all my magic withered up. Then I'll just fester here for evermore. A hanger on. Uncle to my brother's brood of children.

I'll never have children of my own. Never be married. Never find love.

I'm just a shamed vessel. A piranha to society. Hidden away and only good for giving my body and my magic away.

"Are you okay?" asks Colby and his brown eyes are full of concern.

I plaster on a smile. "I'm fine. Just feeling a little woozy because I'm ripe." He does not need to hear all my sorrows.

He frowns a little. "Have they found someone for you?"

"Yes, all arranged, a car is picking me up at seven."

Colby doesn't look convinced by my cheer. He is a perceptive little shit.

"Harry can find someone more permanent..."

"No!" I interrupt. "I'm fine, this is fine. I like the freedom. I like not belonging to anybody."

It's my bed and I'll lie in it, whispers a familiar part of myself. Colby insists that what happened to me was not my fault and logically I can see the truth of it. But I can't just switch off all the years of shame. It's not so easy to reconstruct one's entire beliefs about oneself. I still feel as if I was to blame and that the consequences are deserved.

Colby is staring at me intently. He is a vessel too, so he should understand my declaration of freedom. Well, at least better than most people would. Or perhaps he won't get it at all. He loves belonging to my brother and giving him his magic. Maybe he won't understand.

"Do you belong to no one, or to everyone?" he asks.

I suck in a breath. Talk about sucker punch. In an ideal world, it shouldn't be like this for vessels. There should be no belonging at all. We are people, not pets. But it's far from an ideal world. And the cold hard truth is that every month I have to spread my legs for someone so they can take my magic before I explode.

Would giving myself to only one person be better? Do I want the endless parade of strangers and vague acquaintances to end?

I shiver. I'm being dramatic. It's just sex. Meaningless, unimportant sex. The only thing I have to offer the world. And I'm fine with it. I made my peace with it long ago. Nothing needs to change.

"Sorry," says Colby with a wince. "That was an awful thing for me to say."

He looks genuinely remorseful and I hate to think what expression I gave him to cause him to appear so aghast.

"It's fine," I assure him. "It is sweet that you are concerned for me."

He eyes me suspiciously for a moment and then dives into asking my opinion on the prospective surrogates. No doubt thinking that it is as good a distraction as any, as well as allowing him to get what he came here for.

I smile and indulge him. I could do with a distraction, truth be told. In a few short hours, I need to prepare myself for a prince's bed.

Chapter Two

Will

The penthouse is lovely. Floor to ceiling windows display a stunning view of London. The interior is all very modern and chic. I love coming to England.

The man fawning over me, gives yet another unnecessary bow. "Is everything to your satisfaction, Your Highness?"

"Yes, thank you. Everything is quite lovely."

He bows again, and it is a struggle not to roll my eyes.

"Mr. Reynolds will be over at ten a.m tomorrow to go over the protocols for the King's coronation."

"Very well." I nod.

The man licks his lips. What is he hesitating for? A soft knock on the door answers my question. I sense beautiful magic. Its colors vibrant and vivid. Like the northern lights. I turn towards the door in excitement. A ripe vessel. Like no other I have ever sensed before.

My host scurries over and flings the door open. A young man steps inside. His aquamarine eyes meet mine steadily. His dark hair is tied up in an immaculate bun and I yearn to free it and discover how long it is. And then run my hands through it.

"Your Highness, may I introduce James Cambell, younger brother of Duke Sothbridge."

James inclines his head the bare minimum that could be considered polite.

"Pleased to meet you," I say with a grin.

He is gorgeous. His magic tastes divine, and he is of good stock. I think I might be smitten.

"Mr. Cambell can stay and provide you with company, unless you wish to be alone?"

Excitement and sheer delight bubbles through me. "I'd be delighted if Mr. Cambell stayed."

My host literally rubs his hands together in glee. James rolls his eyes. His presence is hypnotizing. I could stand here and stare at him forever. I barely register the host leaving until the door clicks shut behind him.

James's eloquent fingers start undoing the dark jacket of his suit. "So, where do you want to fuck me?"

I feel my eyebrow raise as I meet his intense glare.

Gorgeous. Powerful and enticing magic. High born. And feisty. Scrub being smitten, I think I'm in love.

"How about we have a drink first?" I say.

His fingers still, and the look he gives me is positively ferocious. "As you wish, Your Highness."

A shudder wracks my body. "Please, call me Will." Formality is awful at the best of times. It is positively hideous with someone I'm about to be intimate with.

He gives another barely perceptible nod and I walk over to the drinks cabinet. I sense his surprise that I'm not expecting him to do it, but he says nothing.

"What can I get you?" I ask.

"Whiskey," he answers.

That surprises me, and I hate that it does. The idea that vessels are all girly is ridiculous. Nearly as ridiculous as the thought that all women prefer cocktails and wine over hard liquor.

"May I call you James?" I ask as I hand him his drink.

His entire body tenses. "No."

Okay. My absolute delight at meeting him is starting to wear off. He clearly hates me and I do not know what I have done to deserve such scorn.

He stares at me for a moment, deep into my eyes. I think he reads something there, because his expression softens slightly.

"It's only ever James when I'm in trouble," he says, then he takes a sip of his whiskey. "My name is Jem."

A grin stretches across my face. Jem. It really suits him. And I'm honored he has given me his familiar name.

"It is a pleasure to meet you, Jem," I say with my most winning smile.

He merely raises one perfectly shaped eyebrow. "You sound English." A perfect steer to safer topics of conversation. I don't mind. I want him to feel comfortable with me.

"My mother is English, and I went to school and university here."

Jem nods as if he approves of the explanation. Then he downs the rest of his drink in one efficient gulp. His stunning eyes meet mine again, and suddenly it's hard to breathe. He places his empty glass on an ornate table beside him.

"Can we get on with this?"

Oh, I'm being an idiot. He doesn't want small talk. His magic is brimming. He is so very full, it must be uncomfortable. Of course he is keen to be emptied, and a dark part of me is drooling in avarice at the thought of taking all his delicious magic and making it my own. As well as getting to delight in what looks like a very fine body.

"Of course, my apologies," I say and I gesture towards the far end of the penthouse. It's all loft style, and the bed is only slightly separated from the rest of the space by a short foot long wall.

Jem turns on his heels and strides towards it, causing me to scurry after him. He stops by the large bed. It's impeccably made with crisp white bedding and plump pillows. Jem stares at it as if he has never seen a bed before.

"How may I please you, Your Highness," he says quietly, almost defeatedly.

The formal words twist in my gut. How may I please you. Words a vessel is supposed to say to the mage who is about to empty them. I'm supposed to reply with the name of the position I want him to assume.

I know we only just met and he is here as part of the British hospitality, but it all seems awfully cold.

"Ah...how about Ja-na-nie?" I suggest. Missionary is fairly straightforward, I'm sure he will be happy with that. It's nothing extravagant.

He nods. "Naked?"

"Yes, please." I'm surprised at how calm my voice sounds, given how much my heart is hammering.

His elegant fingers make quick work of his jacket. I watch transfixed as he places it neatly on the back of a chair. His shirt follows and my jaw drops open at the sight of his pierced nipples. He gracefully steps out of his shiny black loafers. Then he swiftly unbuckles his belt, quickly followed by his fly. His belly button is pierced too, with a ruby red jewel that seems to wink at me. He lowers his trousers and pants together and neatly steps out of them, before retrieving them from the floor, folding them and placing them on the chair.

There is a piercing on the end of his cock. A silver barbell. I swallow. I'm pleased his cock is hard, even though it is not personal. It doesn't mean he fancies me. He is ripe, and his body can sense that I'm a mage.

He doesn't look at me as he climbs onto the bed. I watch the long lean lines of his body. He is absolutely gorgeous. Even more so than I suspected. My lungs stutter. My arousal and desire flares.

Jem lies down on his back and stares at the ceiling. His toenails are painted with red glittery polish. His tailored suit is clearly a costume for meeting a prince and I love everything about that. Jem is the most interesting person I have met in forever. I want to get to know him.

My cock throbs, reminding me that I'm standing here, fully clothed and gaping like a fish. I jerk into motion and hurriedly throw all my clothes off, allowing them to rest wherever they land. Now I can crawl eagerly onto the bed.

He tenses as I approach him, but he spreads his legs wide in invitation. The contradictory reactions are confusing. He doesn't seem like the type to be nervous.

I position myself over him and look down. His eyes are closed, his expression blank. His lips look so soft, I long to taste them, but kissing is for lovers. We are here, together, as mage and vessel, as much as I'm craving it were otherwise.

He would have prepared himself for me. As different as he seems, he is still clearly a trained vessel. He used the formal words, he knows the names of the positions. He knows how to be a good vessel.

All I need to do is line my cock up and sink into him.

I take hold of my cock and wriggle closer to him. I look down and ruby red flashes at me, from in between his legs. He is wearing a butt plug that matches his belly button ring. My heart stutters in my chest. This man is going to be the death of me. He is going to kill me with his sex appeal. And I'm all for it.

I gently brush my fingers along the plug. A grimace passes across his face and I pause. He is not using a brace, but I swear if he was, he'd be biting down on it hard, and not in pleasure. Something is making him uncomfortable.

"Would you prefer a different position?" I ask.

He nods sharply without opening his eyes, so I back away to give him room to move. He flips over onto his stomach and settles. His ass is incredible, I've never seen a more perfect sight. Pert and juicy.

I ease forward again and he tenses. I sigh. I can't deny it anymore, not when the truth is so plain to see. Jem isn't in to this.

Disappointment tastes bitter. I was a fool to think he'd want me. He is a gorgeous, powerful young vessel, of course he is going to belong to someone. Nevermind that English vessels are usually wed on their eighteenth birthday.

Why would he want a stranger when he can spend the night in his master's arms? His master who is evidently a jerk for sending Jem here when he so clearly does not want this, but there is not a lot I can do about that.

I move across the bed and sit on the edge.

"You can go," I say sadly.

I can sense his shock and surprise that quickly turns to outrage. He dives off of the bed and throws his underwear on. Black silky panties that I can't believe I didn't notice when he was taking them off.

He bundles the rest of his clothes and his shoes into his arms and marches away from me. I hear a sniff and see his shoulders trembling. I'm chasing after him before I've had a chance to process a single thought.

"Wait!" I say as I grab his shoulder and turn him around. I catch a quick glimpse of tears before he drops his gaze to the floor.

"Why are you crying?"

"Because you are throwing me out!" he snaps.

"Only because I didn't think you wanted to be here," I explain. Is he feeling humiliated? That is the very last thing I wanted. My heart is pounding with the horrifying knowledge that I have upset him. It's the worst feeling in the world.

"I don't want to be here. It's fine. London is stuffed full of mages, I'm sure someone will empty me."

I stare at the soft sheen of his hair, it is the only thing I can see of him with his head bowed like this. Is he really going to leave here and go to some stranger? The mere thought of it is making me feel sick.

"Is your master away?"

"I don't have a master," he huffs. "I'm sent to a different mages bed every time I'm ripe. So don't flatter yourself into thinking you're something different. I don't care that you don't want me, it won't be hard to find someone who does."

A different mage every time? That sounds awful. I mean, I guess some people would think it was fun, but Jem clearly doesn't. I've never heard of a vessel being treated so poorly. Anger starts to coil low in my gut, but I ignore it. It is not an emotion I need right now.

This lovely young man is passed pillar to post, and now like some sick game of pass the parcel, the music has stopped and he is with me. I need to figure out what is best for him.

"So...um, your reluctance isn't personal? It's not me specifically you don't like, it's the situation in general?" I try to clarify. Gods, I hope I'm right. It probably makes me a selfish shit, but I'm the first to admit that I'm far from perfect.

He nods. A jerky, uncoordinated movement that is far different from the way I've already come to know that he moves.

"Then stay, please. I thought you would be happier with someone else, but if that isn't true, I'd be honored if you stayed." I'm practically begging and I don't even care.

A long, silent and tense moment stretches. I can hear the distant hum of traffic but here in the penthouse it is as if time is holding her breath. Jem's magic is radiating off of him. I can't see, smell or taste it, but I can sense it and it is enticing. I want to sink into it, bathe in it and lose myself forever. Selfishly, I hope my mage presence is similarly calling to him. I want him to say yes.

Jem gives a tiny, barely perceptible nod, and I breathe a sigh of relief. Gently, I take the bundle of clothes and shoes from his arms and place them on a coffee table that is beside us.

Now I'm standing naked in front of a practically naked stranger. It should feel an awful lot more awkward than it does, and that's a very interesting thought. I'm sure it is significant.

"How about we don't do this formally?" I suggest.

Jem lifts his head slightly, just enough so that I can see his brilliant eyes. The look he is giving me is pure unadulterated skepticism.

"We could pretend that we are just doing it for fun," I continue.

He continues to stare at me as if I've completely lost my mind.

"Come on," I say brightly. "If we had met in a club, what would we be doing now?" Not all vessels are gay, but I'm pretty sure Jem is. And I know I'm not ugly.

Jem scowls and his eyes blaze. "We wouldn't meet. I'd be sucking you off through a glory hole."

A wave of arousal dances along my veins. Jem is all but bristling, and his glare is pure belligerence, but if his words were met to put me off, or shock and disgust me, he has really missed the mark. By miles.

"You like glory holes?" I ask, letting the excitement sound in my voice.

He blinks at me, and watching his fierce expression slowly drain away to be replaced by bewilderment is the most endearing thing I've ever seen. He nods warily, as if he is not quite sure where this is going.

"Perfect," I say.

I walk over to the short wall that separates the bed area. It's got to be only a thin stud wall. Merely decorative. At least, I bloody well hope so. I add a discreet blast of magic to my punch, just in case. My fist flies through the wall with no problem. Plaster and dust scatter.

Jem's eyes are huge, and his mouth is open. "Are you crazy?"

I shrug and give him my best malevolent grin. "It's not like I can't afford the repairs."

He blinks slowly. "I guess."

While he is processing that, I position myself on the other side of the wall. I'll take the side with the bits of broken plaster on the floor. Looks like I gauged it just right and the hole is at dick height when I'm standing. Thank heavens. That could have been extremely embarrassing.

Now I just have to stand here with my nose pressed up against a wall and hope that Jem takes the bait. My cock is not the most attractive thing to look at, but what man's is. It's a perfectly acceptable size and right now, rock hard. I'm pretty sure it has been hard since the moment I first laid eyes on Jem.

I'm straining to hear the slightest sound. I think that is soft footsteps approaching. He moves quieter than a cat, if that is him. But it's probably just my wishful thinking.

Something warm and wet licks up the underside of my cock. The yelp that escapes me is unholy. It's part surprise and a whole lot of joy. My hips press flush against the wall, I'm desperate to present as much of myself as I can.

Long, languorous licks continue to torment me. It's hard not to rise up onto my toes. He swirls around my slit and I groan. That feels so damn good.

My palms flatten against the smooth wall. I'd much rather be running my hands through his hair, but this is hot. I can't see him. I can't really hear him. No other parts of our bodies are touching. It's just his tongue and my cock.

I have to imagine him, on the other side of the wall, on his knees. I pray that one day I get to see the sight for real. But in this moment, for some reason, imagining it and not being able to see it feels like the sexiest experience of my life.

A loud carnal cry escapes me as my cockhead is enveloped in soft wet heat. Jem suckles on me gently and I'm seeing stars. He is damn good at this. Plump lips start to slide down my shaft as he takes me deeper. I'm in heaven. The suction, the heat, the moisture. It's all a cacophony of sensations that are overwhelming me.

Now he is moving, adding delicious friction to the waves of pleasure that are consuming me. I wish I could see his head bobbing. I wish this stupid wall wasn't in the way so that he could take all of me. And paradoxically I'm glad the wall is here, something about the enforced separation is lighting up my world.

My impending release is already building. It's gathering strength like an ominous storm. I have to step away. I can't cum like this. Jem is very, very full of magic and I need to be inside his ass to empty him. But I'm not sure I have the willpower.

Somehow, I manage it. I stagger backwards from the wall with a gasp. Then I all but run the few steps it takes to walk around it.

Jem looks beautiful on his knees. He looks up at me. His lips are all swollen and puffy. His eyes wide and dark with lust. He looks a little dazed and his cheeks are tinged pink. He really truly loves giving head. My cock throbs.

Gently, I help him stand before leading him over to the bed. I smoothly push him down onto it, and on to his back.

He looks stunning against the snow-white sheets.

"May I kiss you?" I whisper.

He shakes his head.

"May I kiss your neck?"

His eyes cloud with confusion but he gives a slight nod. So I pounce. I pepper his neck with gentle kisses. Then I lower my head and kiss a trail across his chest. My tongue flicks at one pierced nipple and he gasps. I go lower still, kissing my way down his flat, toned stomach.

He moves up onto his elbows. "Do prince's suck cock?" He sounds incredulous.

I don't stop my downward journey. "This one does," I murmur.

I hesitate a moment, in case he is going to tell me no. But the only sound is his rapid breathing. So I lick the very tip of him and he bucks up off the bed. I love the feel of his piercing against my tongue. It rasps against me as I slide down his length. He makes a soft noise that sings directly to my cock.

I lose myself in the delight of him until his cock pulses in my mouth. He is very, very close.

Reluctantly, I pull off of him with a wet plop. Damn magic. We really need to get to the main event. Tomorrow night when he is not ripe, I'm going to play with him for hours and discover all the noises he makes.

I glance up at him. His eyes are scrunched up tight, but his jaw is slack with pleasure. I gently brush my fingers over his butt plug. He moans. I grin and gently work it out. His hips twitch.

Should I ask him if he wants to roll over? He was happier in that position earlier, but he seems in the zone now and I don't want to snap him out of it by asking him a question and forcing him to engage his thinking brain.

Carefully, I lean over him. I brush my cock over his entrance and he gasps and throws back his head. Definitely in the zone now.

I ease into him. His hole is oiled and opened from the plug. I sink into his warm, tight heat easily. He cries out and clenches around me. This isn't going to take long, for either of us.

He is panting and writhing beneath me now. Utterly beautiful. His body surrenders to mine, stretches around me and accepts me.

I thrust gently, and he keens. I thrust again and again. A soft, sure rhythm. Aiming for his prostate with each slide.

Suddenly his body goes rigid. His hole clamps deliciously around my cock. I watch, completely mesmerized as he cums. His back arches off of the bed. He is lost in his passion and joy. He is so damn beautiful.

His magic rushes into me. A great, overwhelming torrent of it. Like a dam suddenly releasing. His magic is incredible. Iridescent and potent. Gasping, I fall onto the bed next to him. The magic swirls within me. I feel bloated. Too full. I take deep breaths and wait for it to settle.

Beside me, I'm dimly aware of Jem leaving the bed. Many vessels like to clean up immediately after.

His magic pulses within me. Slowly mixing with my own. His is all shades of electric blue and neon green. Mine is golden. The colors clash. But they are slowly coalescing. Forming into a bright swirling entity. Like the surface of a bubble but far stronger.

Another deep breath. Wow, that was a hell of a rush. I've never experienced anything so intense. I've had the pleasure of emptying vessels before, but nothing has come close to this.

I open my eyes and lift my head. It's too dark. Too quiet. I think I drifted for far longer than I thought. It is the still quiet of the small hours of the night. The still quiet of an empty penthouse.

Jem has left. I am alone.

Chapter Three

Jem

I'm not even tasting this pasta salad, but I'm sure it's good. Lottie is a great cook and I love everything she makes. But instead of enjoying it, I'm just sitting here in the breakfast room, consumed by memories of last night. I can still feel the imprint of Will's touch all along my body. As if he has marked me. Or as if his ghost is caressing my flesh.

My thoughts and emotions are all over the place. It was supposed to be just another night. I'm not impressed that he is a prince, all he did to achieve that was to be born. But there is something special about him. I can't deny that.

He is younger than I expected. And far more good-looking. He didn't behave the way I'm used to. He was kind, considerate. He looked at me like I was something far more than a tool for him to use and enjoy.

Then that whole business with the glory hole was quite something. I won't be forgetting that in a hurry. The memory is burned into my brain.

Harry walks into the room, and I bite back my groan. I thought he had already had lunch. He sees me and stops. Tension tightens my spine. I'm really not in the mood for an interrogation right now. I want to be alone with my thoughts, especially since they are mostly dirty ones.

"How was last night?" he asks.

"Do you want all the details, a step-by-step account?" I snap.

He holds my glare unflinchingly. "Of course not, Jem. I just want to know if you are okay."

"I'm fine. Why wouldn't I be?"

Harry sighs heavily. "Did he treat you well?"

I hate the look of concern in his eyes. I hate the pity and his blasted guilt. I miss the old Harry. My brother before he was married. When he didn't care, or he at least thought I deserved my fate. This...sympathy, is awful. Especially as on this occasion it feels entirely undeserved.

"Everything is fine," I say as I storm out of the room.

I flee to my rooms and flop down on my bed. Thoughts of Will immediately crowd my mind again. He did treat me well. Very well. Gave me my first ever blow job for a start. Now I know why everyone goes so mad for them. They feel incredible.

Then the sex was...different. I thought I enjoyed sex, I always cum. Everyone says vessels always do, it is our magic's way of seeking freedom. I thought I was different. Thought I enjoyed it much more than most.

But last night...I can't even finish that thought. Last night was something else entirely. Every other time I have had sex, the pleasure felt mechanical, purely physical. The rubbing of a cock inside me triggered a reaction. But last night - I swear I felt that in my soul. The pleasure swept through my mind and not just my body.

And my magic soared. I've never been emptied so thoroughly. Never left so utterly sated.

It has left me not knowing what to think. Now I'm lost at sea without a compass. I've always been naughty, sexy Jem. Rule breaker, hedonist. But now it seems I was wrong all along. Sex was something I tolerated. It was a necessity. A means to an end, and I stole what meager pleasure I could from it.

And confusingly, I think I might actually be a slut. If what Will showed me was real sex. If that is how it is supposed to feel, I really, truly want more of it. So in a way, I was right about myself all along.

I know I enjoy the power of being sexy, that's for sure. I like being desired. The look in men's eyes when they crave me is electrifying. The look in Will's eyes lit up my world. It seemed to ignite something within me.

I sigh and rub my face. This is beyond confusing.

I thought I liked sex before, but I was wrong, but now I really do like sex and I love that Will desires me? Is that the best conclusion I can come to?

Of course, the fact that Will is incredibly handsome doesn't hurt. My heart does a strange flutter in my chest. Great, heart disease is the last thing I need. Though I'd take that over stupid emotions, any day.

So what if Will looks like my dream man? Tall, dark and handsome personified. It's not like I'm ever going to see him again. He is only in the country for the coronation. He will be home by the time I'm next ripe and it's not like he'd ask for me anyway.

To him, I'm just a vessel. Something that was provided as hospitality, along with champagne and a penthouse. He treated me better than mages normally do, but that is probably just him. He probably treats everyone well. The type of man who remembers the names of the spouses of all his staff and sends them birthday gifts.

"Jem!" shrieks Colby as he bounds into my bedroom without knocking. I swear he is the most annoying brother-in-law on the face of the planet. If he didn't make my brother so happy, I'd be plotting against him.

"There is a prince here to see you!" he exclaims with wide, frantic eyes.

I sit up swiftly. What the hell? My heart is hammering and my body is trembling. My mind is scrambling for purchase but nothing makes sense, so there is nothing to cling onto. I'm in freefall.

"Oh my god, oh my god, I can't remember the protocol for hosting a prince! I need to phone my mother!" With that, Colby turns tail and runs out of my room. Leaving me alone and shaking.

Will is here? He tracked me down? What on earth is he thinking? Maybe it's bad and I offended him and he has come to berate Harry about my behavior? No, wait. Colby said he was here to see me, not Harry.

I stagger over to the mirror. My hair is a mess. I'm wearing a plain tee shirt and jeans. Does he expect me to dress up for him? Should I try to throw something together?

When he has turned up unannounced? Well, sod him. I don't owe him a thing. If he wants to barge into my home and demand to see me, he can see me as I am.

So why is it so hard to move my feet towards the door?

Chapter Four

Jem

By the time I make my way downstairs, everyone is in the best parlor drinking tea from the very best china, because of course they are.

Harry looks completely unruffled, while Colby looks like he is shaking. There is a giant mountain of a man lurking by the door, who I can only assume is Will's bodyguard.

"Jem! I mean, James! You are here!" babbles Colby. He looks so nervous, I wouldn't be surprised if he fainted.

Will turns his head in my direction, and it looks like his whole face lights up when he sees me. He politely gets to his feet, and now I feel like an ass for slouching down in my casual clothes, after dithering about it for an age.

Everyone else is dressed smartly. Will's suit clings to the contours of his body. I try to swallow but my mouth is too dry. His magic pulses around him, like an aura. His gold tones are swirling with my green and blue. My magic is flavoring his own. It is a little disorientating.

His smile is beaming, and his eyes sparkling as he engulfs my hand in a warm handshake. The feel of his skin upon mine nearly makes me shiver. I give a very slight incline of my head, only because Colby will have a nervous breakdown if I don't.

Then suddenly I'm sitting at the table, having tea with my one-night stand from last night and my brother, and brother-in-law. Just perfect. My magic swirling through Will is blatant proof that he is the mage that emptied me. There are no secrets here. Harry and Colby know everything.

"We were just talking about the coronation," says Colby, far too brightly.

"Ah, yes. It is tomorrow, isn't it?" I say innocently.

Colby flushes, and a wave of guilt washes over me. It's hardly his fault I'm not invited, I'm being a jerk making him feel bad about it, even though he is not the target of my intentions.

"I assume you have a front-row seat, Your Highness?" I ask sweetly.

I need to put Will in his place, and that place is very much above me. He is a prince. He should not be having tea with a disgraced vessel, even though I'm the son of a duke.

"No, I'm quite far at the back, actually," Will answers jovially.

Damn him. I glare at him, but he seems impervious to my belligerence. He just smiles back at me, as if I'm being nice to him. It is infuriating.

"Are you staying in England for long, Your Highness?" asks Colby.

I give Harry a sharp look. Why is he making his poor husband carry the conversation? But Harry doesn't look at me. His gaze is fixed on Will. To anyone else his expression would look neutral, but I know him, and I know he is pissed off. Furious even. What is his problem?

Oh. I get it. My dear brother rarely meets the mages who empty me. And after the ones he knew, tried to murder Colby, I guess he is feeling a little protective.

Too little, too late. Whispers a dark, disgruntled part of me. I ignore it. Harry has always tried to do his best by me. He is only human, mistakes happen. He is my brother and I love him and that is the only thing that matters.

"I'll be staying for the summer," says Will. "My nephew is about to come of age and inherit his title and as he is a vessel, the vultures are circling."

"You are Barny's uncle?" exclaims Colby. Is there anyone on the planet that he doesn't know?

"Yes I am," says Will with a soft smile.

He is going to be here for the summer. My stupid heart wants to flutter, which is ridiculous. Being in the same country doesn't mean a thing. It doesn't mean I'm going to get to see him again. It certainly doesn't mean he intends to court me, and that is what this blasted tea is about.

"I was wondering if Jem would like to join me at Rocester Hall for the summer?" says Will.

My lungs completely freeze. That's not courting. It's worse, as well as better. Far more intense, but not something one asks of a respectable vessel.

Colby gasps and nearly spills his tea.

"That would not be appropriate," growls Harry with a frown, as if I have any honor left to protect.

"Of course, my apologies. I was thoughtless in my excitement to get to know Jem better. Please forgive me," Will says smoothly.

I can't tell if he is genuinely contrite, or if he is disappointed, or annoyed at being refused. His game face is just too good. I can't tell a thing.

Harry just glares at him and does not accept the prince's apology. It is very rude of him and I love it. There is going to be no fawning from my brother.

"More tea?" squeaks Colby.

He flounders around in small talk with Will, while I try to get my brain cells to function again and recover from their shock. Will wants to spend the entire summer with me? Was I really that good of a lay? I must have been, because there is no other possible explanation for his behavior. Perhaps he has had to leave his usual vessel at home in Bavaria and he needs a substitute for his stay.

My imagination starts to go wild. Spending the summer with Will. All those nights. Would he want me in his bed every night, or just when I was ripe? I hope it is the former, because my cycle is fairly long. I think he is planning the former, I get the distinct impression he really enjoys sex and has a very healthy appetite.

It would be a hell of a way to spend the next few months. Staying somewhere new, regularly getting my guts rearranged by Will. Oh gods. I think I'm blushing. How do I get it to stop? I'll have to stare at my tea for now and pray that no one notices.

It's stupid to get excited by the idea, anyway. Harry has already said no, and it is a stupid, scandalous plan. What was Will thinking?

"I'm afraid I must dash," says Will. "There is a coronation rehearsal I need to attend."

The room fills with the sound of scraping chairs as we all get to our feet.

"I'll see you out," I say.

Will beams in delight at me. Harry frowns, but says nothing. The two mages shake hands, then Will shakes Colby's hand. I turn on my heels and lead Will out of the parlor. His bodyguard trails behind us.

"What the hell are you doing here?" I hiss as soon as we are in the hallway.

"Inviting you to stay with me, but since that was declined, how about a dinner date?"

My feet freeze and take root in the floorboards. I don't know how Will didn't crash into me, but he doesn't. Even his massive bodyguard manages to stop in time.

"What? Why?" I babble inanely.

Will is grinning. "Because I want to spend time with you," he says, as if it is as simple as that.

I know I'm staring. I'm standing here with a daft, vacant expression on my face. I want to move, but my body is rebelling. It's most unfair.

"You do realize I'm disgraced?" I say eventually.

A flash of anger fires in Will's eyes. The sight of it makes me shiver, but I don't think it's fear I'm feeling. And I don't think he is angry at me.

"I don't care," he says simply, and his smile is back.

Mutely, I start walking again. He doesn't care? What kind of nonsense is that? He may be a prince and used to getting whatever he wants, but he is by no means impervious to scandal. In fact, as a prince, he is more susceptible than most. Bavaria can't be that different.

Does he really believe he can swan in here, demand that I go to dinner with him and that there will be no ramifications? Is he so big-headed that he thinks he is above consequences?

"No, I'm not going to dinner with you," I say sternly.

We've reached the front door now. The butler is holding it open and Will's limo is gleaming on the forecourt. The sunlight is bright and dazzling compared to the shade of the house.

Suddenly, Will takes my hand, enveloping it in both of his. His touch is warm and somehow comforting. It makes my insides do strange things.

"Please," he says.

His brown eyes are wide and all but begging. Beneath the puppy dog look, there is the hard steel of determination. This is not a man who takes no for an answer. He is accustomed to getting what he wants and right now, he wants me. What an idiot.

I'm pretty sure Harry will not object to a dinner date, it is perfectly respectable after all. Well, for me at least. For Will, being seen with the likes of me is an entirely different matter.

"One dinner, if you promise to leave me alone afterwards," I say. It seems like I'm going to have to make him see sense while on a date.

His smile is beautiful. His joy makes his eyes sparkle. It's a completely over the top reaction to having dinner with me. The man is insane.

"Deal!" he exclaims. "I'll send a car to collect you at five p.m the day after tomorrow. There is a lovely restaurant not far from here."

"Fine," I grumble as I reclaim my hand from his hold.

"Oh, I also came to return this," he says with a truly evil gleam in his eye.

He reaches into his jacket pocket and pulls out my butt plug. The one set with a fake ruby. He presents it to me as if it is a bouquet of flowers. I snatch it from him and shove it into my pocket. I don't think anyone apart from his bodyguard saw.

"What, you want to check that it fits? Like some filthy version of Cinderella?" I snap.

Will's eyes light up with merriment, and he laughs. Deep and hearty. The sound of it sets butterflies off in my stomach.

"Well, I am a prince and you did run away from me at midnight," he says. "Forcing me to come and find you."

I scowl at him. "I didn't force you to do anything, and you are not Prince Charming."

He takes my hand and bends over it. "I could be your charming prince, if you'd let me," he says and then he brushes his lips across my knuckles.

Fuck him. How dare he pull such a move and make me feel all light-headed and swoony.

He gives me another grin, then turns and bounds down the steps. My heart lurches at the sight of him leaving. It is the most ridiculous feeling I have ever had, and that is saying something.

I watch his car drive away as I pull myself together. It has to be aftereffects of being ripe, or effects of being emptied so thoroughly. I'm not normally so vapid.

"Tell me everything!" demands Colby from right behind me. His sudden appearance makes me nearly jump out of my skin. How did he creep up on me? How long has he been there?

I whirl to face him. His eyes are bright and insistent. Utterly ruthless. There is going to be no escape. I'm doomed.

Oh gods, will this nightmare never end?

Chapter Five

Will

I knew Jem would be late, so I'm not worried. Behind me, I can feel Mark seething at the perceived slight. He is a very overprotective bodyguard. But he needn't worry. I'm quite content to wait. The restaurant is lovely, and the pianist playing in the corner is extremely talented. The art work on the walls is interesting to look at, and the high dome ceiling is stunning. This white wine is delicious to sip on and the bread rolls are a soft delight to nibble on. I'm happy to sit here and enjoy my surroundings for as long as it takes.

The servers keep casting me increasingly anxious glances. They think I've been stood up, and they are worried how I am going to take it. They are wrong, Jem will be here, I know he will.

I'm facing the front door, so I see him the moment he strides in. My lungs forget how to function. My mind lights up, and my cock stirs.

Jem says something to the host, but he doesn't wait to be shown to our table. His eyes have already found mine, as if we are magnetically drawn to one another. He heads my way, walking across the restaurant as if he owns it. The host scurries after him.

His gorgeous hair is loose and I can finally see how long it is. It's shoulder length and falls in soft waves. His very tight red crop top shows off the clear outline of his piercings. His midriff is bare and his belly button jewelry is a golden amber today. I can't help wondering if he is wearing a matching butt plug.

My eyes continue to drift downward, drinking in the sight of him. His tiny shorts are red like his top and the material clings to him beautifully. There is a flash of fishnet tights embracing his thighs before the top of shiny black PVC boots begin. He looks incredible. My mouth is watering. I'm struggling to believe that I've already had the honor of having him in my arms.

He strides up to me and cocks his head to the side. "Still want me to join you?"

I blink. "Of course! Why on earth would I change my mind? Look at how beautiful you are!"

A faint pink tinge colors his cheeks and he shifts uncomfortably, as he looks away. He seems completely bamboozled by my reply and I hate that he was expecting anything different from me, even though it is to be expected. He barely knows me. One night of carnal bliss does not enlighten you to a person's character.

Nevermind the soul chilling, rage inducing fact that no one has treated Jem the way he should be treated.

He has every reason to assume that people, and especially mages, are bastards. I don't blame him at all. I merely hope I get the opportunity to prove to him that not everyone is like that. There are some decent people in the world, and I like to think, while far from perfect, I'm still one of them.

I move around the table and pull the chair out for him. "Please, have a seat."

He flashes me a very flustered and confused look as he takes his seat. A server hurries over and hurriedly fills his glass. Jem picks it up and takes a big gulp of the white wine.

"They will probably throw me out in a minute," he whispers.

"You're my guest, they wouldn't dare," I growl.

Jem just stares at me with that bewildered look he gets and that I find utterly enticing.

"So, now that you've shown me that you are slutty trash and that I shouldn't want to be seen with you, and I've shown you that I think you are wrong, shall we order?"

His eyes widen and his mouth drops open. Then he blushes, drops his gaze and fumbles for his wine.

"Am I really so obvious," he mumbles.

"Yes," I answer.

His gaze snaps back to mine. His eyes flash with anger for a brief moment, and then he huffs out a soft laugh. The sound is musical and light and it dances its way into my soul where I want to keep it forever. Jem laughing is the most beautiful sound in the whole wide world. I need to hear more of it.

"Fair cop," he says. "You got me. I'll try my best to be civil for the rest of the evening."

A server steps up and Jem orders in effortless French, including instructions on just how much sauce he wants on the dish. He also orders another bottle of wine. A very good wine. The server casts me a nervous glance and I nod. If Jem saw that, he is choosing to ignore it.

I stumble my way through my order. And the server takes our menus and hurries off.

Jem knows his food, wine and French. Every new thing I learn about him, makes me crush on him even harder. He is quite simply wonderful.

"How was the coronation?" he asks. A nice, polite topic. He really has switched to his best behavior.

"Dull," I say. "I kept waiting for someone to trip or fudge up their words, or something. But no, sadly it all went smoothly."

Jem grins at me. "I can't believe they had to read their lines from paper, come on, they had one job, biggest of their life and they couldn't memorize a few words?"

"Sounds like watching it on the telly gave you a better view than I had," I say with a wry smile.

He smiles back and takes another sip of wine. "Probably."

Out of the corner of my eye, I can see that the other restaurant customers are staring. How very rude of them. I hope it's not making Jem feel uncomfortable. I'd offer him my jacket but it would only seem as if I want him to cover up, when nothing could be further from the truth. I am exulting in the view, and people should be able to wear whatever the hell they want to, without being judged by narrow-minded assholes.

"Was there an after party?" asks Jem, and it takes a moment to recall what we were talking about.

"Not one I was invited to," I say. "Which is a relief because it meant I could escape back to the penthouse and watch the Manchester City versus Leeds game."

"Which side do you support?" asks Jem.

"Man City," I say with a grin.

"Correct answer," says Jem as he lifts his wineglass to his lips. He gives me a wink and I nearly die. My nervous system spins into chaos. His sexiness overloads my brain. My stomach twists, my muscles tremble, my heart speeds up.

This is going to be the best dinner date in the history of the universe.

Chapter Six

Jem

Colby pounces on me the very second I step through the door.

"How did it go!" he gushes, all but hopping foot to foot in his excitement.

His brown eyes are wide and puppy dog bright. To look at him, you'd think that me going on a date is the most exciting thing to have ever happened to him.

"It was fine," I say calmly.

Colby exhales and puts his hands on his hips. "I was watching you on the security feed as you were walking up the steps. You were *smiling*!"

I glare at him. I smile. It's not a rare thing. I don't think so, anyway. Even if it was, there is absolutely no need for him to make a big deal out of it. And he shouldn't have been spying on me in the first place.

I try to ignore Colby and walk past him, towards my rooms, but he just follows me.

"Come on, Jem. Please! I've never been on a date. I want to know all about it."

That piece of information is surprising. Did Harry and Colby really not meet up at all before their arranged marriage? Though thinking about it, it does sound exactly like the type of thing old Harry would have done.

"My brother takes you out all the time," I say. And it's true. It's probably Harry's way of trying to make amends.

"That's not the same and you know it!" persists Colby.

Annoyingly, I have to agree that he has a point. Dinner with your husband isn't exactly a date. Maybe I should offer a swap? Because dinner with my husband is not something I am ever going to experience.

We reach my rooms and I flop down on my sofa. Colby invites himself to sit down next to me. I ignore him and pull off my boots. They are gorgeous, but comfort really isn't one of their strong points. I wriggle my toes and flex my ankles as I sigh in relief.

Colby is staring at me expectantly. I groan in defeat. I'm a sucker for those puppy dog eyes. In my defense, it is probably those eyes that have my once formidable brother wrapped around Colby's finger. If Harry is powerless before this imploring look, how am I supposed to resist?

"What do you want to know?"

Colby literally jumps up and down in his seat with glee. "Everything, where did you go, what was he wearing, what did you eat, what did you talk about, did he pull your chair out for you?"

I stare at him in horror. Does he really want to know all that? He stares back at me as if he hasn't just given me an incredibly long list of demands.

Then just as I open my mouth to speak, he all but shrieks, "Do you like him? That's the most important part!"

I shake my head at Colby. "It doesn't matter if I like him or not."

"Oh! That means you do!" says Colby with a deeply satisfied look in his eyes.

I frown at him. How can one person be so annoying?

"Are you going to spend the summer with him?"

Has my brother-in-law completely lost his mind? "Harry already said no," I say slowly and carefully, as if speaking to a small child.

Colby's brows furrow for a moment, then his eyes widen and he slaps his hand over his mouth. "Oh, my goodness. I can't believe I still get shocked by how old-fashioned you guys are! Harry does not own you, Jem! If you want to go, I will remind Harry of that fact."

Now my stomach is twisting, and my heart is doing strange things. Is this what hope feels like? Do I want to spend the summer with Will? All these possibilities are dizzying.

"People used to be scared of my brother," is what I grumble instead of saying any of that.

Colby grins, entirely free of remorse. "The right people still are."

"And we are not old-fashioned, you are entirely too progressive," I add.

He merely grins some more and pats my knee. "Now, did you have a nice time tonight?"

The change of topic catches me off guard, and to my horror I feel a smile stretching across my face. One I am powerless to stop. Colby chuckles in delight and I want to die of mortification.

I did have a nice time. A wonderful time. Will is lovely company, and he treats me like a person, not just a dumb vessel. Bavaria must be very different. But I'm still a disgrace and he is still a prince. Unless his country won't care if a vessel becomes part of his household for the summer? Perhaps being disgraced is so lowly in their eyes, that it wouldn't be a problem. I would just be something their prince used during his stay in England. Like borrowing a manservant or butler.

A soft knock on the door interrupts my thoughts.

"Come in," I call.

Chris walks in carrying a slim glass vase filled with six perfect blood-red roses. Oh, my god! This cannot be happening. Who on earth sends flowers anymore? And to a disgraced vessel? What the hell is Will thinking?

Colby squeals and jumps off of the sofa. He clearly thinks this latest development is nothing short of fantastic. But then again, he is treating this whole thing as his own personal soap opera.

"These were just delivered for you, Mr. Cambell. I took the liberty of placing them in a vase."

"Thank you, Chris. Can you place them on the dresser please?"

Chris does as I ask and then quietly leaves. I look up at Colby who is furiously scrolling on his phone.

"Found it!" he exclaims. "Six roses mean, the sender is infatuated and wants the receiver to be theirs!"

He strolls over to the small bouquet and starts examining the flowers intently.

I blink at him. I have no idea what to say. I have no idea what to think. This is insane. My palms are sweaty and my heart is beating far too fast. I really need to schedule a cardiac check up.

"Oh, there is no note," says Colby, with disappointment clear in his voice. He turns to look at me. "I wouldn't have read it! I would just have passed it to you!"

I still can't speak. All I can do is sit here helplessly. Colby seems to discern my predicament, and he comes and sits beside me again, with a kind smile. He pats my knee and looks me deep in the eye.

"Shall I tell Harry that you are going to Rocester Hall for the summer?"

My thoughts are all over the place. My emotions are a tangled mess, but my body nods.

Colby grins in triumph. His face is a picture of delight. There will be no backtracking now. Looks like I'm spending the summer with Will.

Chapter Seven

Will

This sweeping driveway up to Rocester hall is impressive. Up ahead, the house itself looks beautiful in the early morning light. All red brick and grand window arches, surrounded by verdant green formal gardens.

A pang of guilt shivers through me. This should not be my first time here. This was my sister's marital home. She may be happily married to someone else now, but all the years she lived here, I never once visited.

And I've hardly been present in my nephew's life at all. I should have stepped up more when his father died. I need to do better. My busy schedule is not an excuse.

As soon as my car stops at the bottom of the steps to the front entrance, a smartly dressed footman opens the car door whilst giving a precise bow.

Then the butler greets me as I step into the morning sunshine. "Welcome to Rocester Hall, Your Highness."

My magic senses prickle at the power emanating from the butler. That's surprising. Old Blood rarely choose staff who have magic of their own. Something else teases at my perception. A vague sense that this man is not entirely human.

The butler is a physically striking man. Tall and slender, but with definite definition under his immaculate black suit. His eyes are black, not just dark, but actually coal black. They are striking against his pale skin, though there is a tinge of color to his skin tone that may hint at some Asian ancestry. His hair is jet black and choppy. It reminds me of the type of haircuts Kpop idols have. I can't discern his age. He has one of those faces that is impossible to tell. He could be anything from twenty to fifty.

I certainly can't tell what non-human blood he has, and it is rude to ask, so I guess it is going to remain a mystery.

"Please allow me to introduce myself, my name is Jeeves and should you require anything at all during your stay, please do not hesitate to inform me."

"A pleasure to meet you, Jeeves," I say with my best smile. "I sent a message ahead saying that I will be having a guest stay with me."

"All received, Your Highness," says Jeeves smoothly.

"If it is not too much trouble, could my guest be placed in a bedchamber close to mine?" I ask.

Jeeves gives me a soft, all-knowing smile. "Would a chamber with a connecting door to yours suffice?"

"Perfect," I grin.

I really am getting ahead of myself. Jem only agreed to stay, nothing else, but there is no harm in making preparations. The connecting door can stay firmly shut for his entire visit, though I sincerely hope it won't.

"Your entourage arrived a short while ago and your things have been placed in your chambers, please allow me to show you the way."

I nod at Jeeves and follow him into the house.

"Master Barnaby sends his apologies for being too unwell to greet you," says Jeeves.

"Oh, I do hope he feels better soon," I say automatically as concern spikes through me. Is he really sick or does he not want to see me?

"Very kind of you, Your Highness. I suspect Master Barnaby will feel well enough this afternoon, once he has slept off last night's excess."

A grin spreads across my face. Well, that's a relief. As well as enlightening. My nephew is a bit of a party animal. I was a bit of a hellion in my younger days, so I can certainly relate. As well as feel a little proud. Vessels are far too often raised to be meek little things. It's a relief to know that has not been Barny's fate. It's a sad but true fact that he is going to have to be Earl Rocester first, and a vessel second. Otherwise there are far too many mages who would relish the opportunity to swoop in, marry him and become the de facto earl. Which is exactly what I am here to prevent.

Jeeves shows me to some absolutely splendid rooms. They are so lovely, I suspect they are the master rooms and poor Barny has been evicted for my stay. Experience has taught me that the only thing I can do is graciously accept and say nothing. People hear the words prince, and lose their minds. No matter what I do to try to dissuade them otherwise.

"Is everything to your satisfaction, Your Highness?"

"Yes, very much so, thank you Jeeves."

Jeeves gives me an eloquent bow and silently leaves. As soon as I am alone, I look at my watch. At least five whole hours until Jem is due to arrive. My heart sinks. It's going to be the longest, dullest day of my entire life. When really I should just be ecstatic that Jem agreed to come, and I'm going to see him later. Despite all evidence to the contrary, I am a grown man and not an over excited toddler.

I sigh wearily at myself. Five hours and then I get to spend the entire summer with Jem. Hopefully, he and Barny will get along and we can all have a merry time. It will be good for Barny to meet another vessel. Especially an unmarried one. Not that Jem's life seems like something to aspire to, but it will be good for Barny to see that there are options. It's not just eternal virginity or marriage, regardless of what society claims.

Thinking about Jem's situation sours my mood. Part of me is itching to know why he is treated so poorly. And I despise that part of me, because Jem is entitled to his privacy, and whatever the fuck happened, I know damn well that Jem does not deserve to be treated the way he is. Wanting to know the details is just grotesque nosiness. I should mind my own business. Besides, the facts will probably only serve to throw me into a blind rage anyway.

Jem is going to be here for the summer, that is all that matters. I can show him how he deserves to be treated, if he will let me. If not, I can at the very least stop him being passed around like a parcel.

For a few months.

An icy trickle runs down my spine. Summers are short, and then I will be returning to Bavaria, and Jem to his fate. My stomach churns. I already hate that thought. How much worse is it going to feel once I know Jem so much better, after I've spent an entire season with him?

I shiver and pull myself together. There will be plenty of time to cross that bridge when we come to it. It's a problem for future me to deal with. Now me, just gets to enjoy himself and have a good time.

My sour mood drifts away and I feel in good cheer once more. Time to explore Rocester Hall. That should kill a few hours while I'm waiting for Jem.

Chapter Eight

Jem

As Rocester hall sweeps into view, I'm struck by another wave of nerves that leaves me trembling. What was I thinking? I'm regretting this already and I'm barely in the driveway. I've been dropped off at all sorts of places to be emptied, and I usually don't give a shit. It takes a few hours at most and then I'm driven home again.

This feels monumentally different. I've never been invited to stay before. Never been wanted for my body and not just my magic. Which I am fairly certain is what Will wants. I am pretty certain it is what I want too. A long dirty summer. But I've never even done a dirty weekend before, so this is quite the leap. A definite step outside of my comfort zone, but isn't that supposed to be a good thing?

Oh no! The driver is pulling up by the front entrance. Surely I should use the back entrance, like the dirty little secret that I am? This is awful.

Is that Will bounding down the steps to greet me? Oh my gosh, shoot me now! Has he forgotten that he is a prince? Well, there is no one here to see, I suppose. That's something at least.

I clamber ungracefully out of the car. For a moment, it looks like Will is about to hug me, but he pulls up short and offers his hand instead. He engulfs my hand in a far too vigorous handshake, that shakes my entire body.

"Jem!" he exclaims. "You made it! How was your journey?"

I raise an eyebrow. He is acting as if I crossed a dangerous mountain pass to get here, and not merely spent a few hours on the M5 in the back of a Rolls-Royce.

"It was fine," I mutter.

"Come! Let me give you the tour!"

He still hasn't released my hand, and he uses it to tow me after him. We reach the front door and I nearly walk into him when he stops suddenly. He pulls me forward to stand beside him and I find myself blinking at a young man.

"Welcome to Rocester Hall, Mr. Cambell. I'm Lord Rosewarne, but please call me Barny."

Oh yes, the soon to be Earl Rocester. The master of the house I'm staying in. I shake his hand. He is being very polite to his uncle's bit of fun.

"Thank you for having me," I say.

He smiles at me and something almost parental ignites within me. His smile is shy, almost unsure. His baby blue eyes look a little sad and a whole lot lonely. His mop of golden hair is cute, and he is overall gorgeous. I can feel his untapped magic tingling along my skin. It's potent. He has the potential to be an extremely powerful vessel. Fuck.

Young, beautiful, powerful, an earl in his own right. Will was right about vultures. There are going to be wolves too. Every sort of predator is going to want him. How is Will going to fight them all off?

Before I can say another word, Will is pulling me after him again and rambling about the architecture of the house. Anyone would think he was stupidly excited to see me.

After showing me the entire house whilst talking incessantly, he flings open a door to a beautiful set of rooms.

"I hope you will be comfortable in here," says Will.

Oh my. I know mistress rooms when I see them. These rooms adjoin the master rooms, if I'm not mistaken. And I'd bet good money that there is a small, discreet door in the bedchamber that leads directly to his.

I fight a losing battle against a blush that is taking over my face. I'm being ridiculous. I'm not shy and I know damn well what I'm here for. Will may be lovely and he may send roses, but he still only wants one thing. And I came here because I'm happy to give it to him. I want to explore the type of sex he showed me. Getting all flustered about it is absurd.

"I'll leave you to get settled in and I'll see you at dinner?" he says.

There is concern in his brown eyes. Seems he has picked up on my sudden and irrational discomfort. I guess my stupid blushing gave me away.

"That sounds lovely," I say with my best false smile.

Will smiles softly and leaves. His absence feels like a burn and I want to chase after him. There is something seriously wrong with me. Where are these strange urges coming from? Thankfully, I'm able to stop myself from following them.

I take a deep breath. Okay, I need to shower, change and pull myself together before dinner. It's just dinner, it will be fine. There is no need to be nervous.

Okay, I surrender. I admit it. I'm not nervous, I'm terrified. Sitting here at dinner is beyond awful. I was sixteen when I was disgraced, and while Colby has included me in all the social events he has hosted at home, this is my first event somewhere else, and neither Colby nor Harry are with me. I'm all alone. I'm out of my depth and I'm drowning.

It's just dinner, but right now, I swear I can't remember which fork is which. And what kind of duke's son doesn't know basic table manners? They are all going to be staring at me and wondering what the hell is wrong with me. I'm too scared to look up from my plate and see, but I just know that is what's happening.

Will and Barny are making polite small talk but I haven't been able to join in. My mind is blank and I can't think of a single thing to say. Will is going to ask me something in a minute, just to include me, I know he is. I'm going to make a complete idiot of myself. My mouth and throat feel far too dry to talk for a start.

Who knew I was such a baby? I'm bitterly disappointed in myself. All those years I said I didn't care that I was not invited anywhere, not even to my own brother's wedding, I was right. I shouldn't have cared, because look at what happens to me when I am invited. I fall to pieces. I can't even handle one little dinner, with two whole people. Two very nice people at that.

My fork clangs noisily against my plate, and the room falls silent. It is so hard not to squirm in my seat, but I think I'm managing it.

"Jem, are you alright?" asks Will.

"I'm fine, I just have a headache." Oh, sweet inspiration! "In fact, if you would excuse me, I am going to retire."

Will gets to his feet. "I'll walk you to your rooms."

Oh fuck.

Chapter Nine

Will

We walk silently through the hallways. I'm at a loss as to what has got Jem so anxious and agitated. It can't be Barny, the boy is extremely unthreatening. The butler is a bit creepy, but I swear Jem hasn't even noticed him.

I don't think it is Mark, because Jem seemed completely unphased by him, both at his home and at the restaurant. And my bodyguard has had the sense to stay in the dining room.

It's certainly a puzzle and I don't like not knowing what the problem is, because if I don't know what it is, I can't fix it. But I can't exactly interrogate Jem. That probably wouldn't help at all.

We reach the door to his rooms, and Jem looks up at me.

"Do you want to come in?" he says softly.

Excitement tingles down my spine. Is this what he was nervous about? Inviting me in? Jem doesn't strike me as the shy sort and I'm pretty sure that it's blatantly obvious that I'm going to say yes. Surely there is no room for fear of rejection?

"I'd be delighted to," I say with a grin.

Jem nods and opens the door. He leads me straight to the bedchamber and his fingers start fumbling with the buttons of his shirt. I can't tear my eyes away.

"I've never done this before," he croaks.

"Done what?" I ask, startled out of my hypnotic daze.

"Have sex without being ripe," he says in a rush. "Well, I did it once, but that was..." he trails off and starts trembling and breathing in fast shallow, frantic breaths.

Concern flashes through me. I place my hands over his, to stop his undressing. His beautiful eyes are wide. I don't like seeing him like this.

"We don't have to have sex, Jem," I say as gently as I can. I sincerely hope this is not the problem, but I have to make it clear, just in case it is.

He stares at me. "But...but that is what I'm here for."

Cold horror fills my veins and settles like ice in my stomach. Does Jem really think this of me? That I brought him here merely to use for my own personal pleasure? And surely he doesn't believe that I would demand sex from him, as some sort of payment for him being my guest? Some twisted privilege I get to invoke because I was born a prince?

But looking at his wide eyes and far too pale face, it is clear that he does. My heart sinks.

"Let's have a drink," I suggest.

I steer Jem into the sitting room and gently push him down onto a chaise lounge. Then I head over to the drinks cabinet. I pour us a whiskey each and sit next to him. He takes his drink and lifts it to his lips. The whiskey sloshes gently from his trembling hand.

His words from a few moments ago have been rattling around inside my skull and now my mind is finally processing them. Jem has never had sex without being ripe. Apart from one time that was clearly traumatic. Why has he chosen to live his life like this? Is this why he likes glory holes, it is the only pleasure he allows himself?

Actually, thinking about it, is it a choice at all? Has Jem been ordered to only share his body when told to? Sex can throw a vessel's cycle off. It's not improbable that his keepers want his cycle to be nice and regular, to make pimping him out easier to arrange.

Jem takes another shaky sip of his whiskey. I'm close enough that I can smell him. Some nice fruity body spray and beneath that a scent that is his own. Clean skin and something that is just Jem. It is intoxicating.

My emotions are a tangled, conflicting storm. Anger, disgust, sorrow, hurt and a deep insidious desire. I'm an animal. Wanting Jem when he is so clearly upset, is abhorrent.

I take a deep breath and carefully choose my words before I speak.

"I'd love to have sex with you again, Jem. But it's not a condition of being my guest. I invited you here, because I want to get to know you better, and yes, I am hoping that will lead to us being intimate. But I am not going to demand it of you."

Jem's dazzling eyes are staring deep into my own. I can almost see him struggling to digest what I have said. And it hurts. He really thinks I'm an asshole.

No, wait. I am being an asshole. I'm making it all about me and taking it personally. When, from what I have gleaned about Jem's life, I know damn well he has every reason to expect the worst from people. It's not about me at all. It's all about Jem's past experiences. I already knew this. Getting offended is childish of me.

"Okay," Jem says slowly. He sounds confused.

I get to my feet and Jem flows to his. I'm happy to see that his usual grace is returning.

"I'll leave you in peace now, but I look forward to seeing you at breakfast," I say.

I hope it's clear that I'm only leaving to give him some space and I'm very much looking forward to spending more time with him. I don't want Jem to think I'm angry with him, or disappointed, or heaven's forbid, disgusted by his mini freak out.

He politely escorts me to the door. I stand in the doorway and turn back to face him. He still looks dazed. A strand of his dark hair has escaped his bun. I reach out and gently tuck it behind his ear. His breath hitches a little and he leans towards my touch. My lungs freeze and my heart rate triples. He does want me.

"May I kiss you?" I whisper.

Jem's dazzling aquamarine eyes darken with desire as he stares unflinchingly into my eyes. Anticipation zaps along my skin, but Jem softly shakes his head. Disappointment tastes bitter, but it's not the end of the world. I have the whole summer to convince Jem to kiss me.

"Goodnight," I breathe.

"Goodnight," repeats Jem softly, still staring at me as if he is trying to read my soul. I hope he is seeing good things.

I shut the door softly and force my body to walk away. I already can't wait for breakfast.

Chapter Ten

Jem

Will is a dangerous man. I came down to breakfast and found him waiting for me with a huge picnic hamper and a beaming smile, and now I'm sitting under a willow tree by a babbling brook, having a picnic in the gentle morning sunlight.

Who has a picnic for breakfast? I have never heard of such a thing. But I have to admit that it is lovely. It's not hot yet, and the air is crisp and clean, still clinging to the chill of night. There are not even that many bugs around. And this spot is divine. Never mind that croissants make perfect picnic food. Delicious, easy to eat, and devouring them outside means there is no need to worry about crumbs. The ants can deal with those.

Add the energizing freshly squeezed orange juice, and I'm feeling as if all is well with the world. I'm very curious about what else is in the hamper, but I can wait.

Will is waffling on about something or other. I love the timbre of his voice, I could listen to it all day. I know he won't mind that I'm not paying much attention, I can tell he is talking to fill the silence and put me at ease. I especially love that he is acting as if last night never happened. Bless him.

It is embarrassing enough that I fell apart like that, I certainly do not need to be reminded of the fact. Pretending it never happened is the perfect solution.

"Apparently Barny is having a party tonight and they get quite rowdy," says Will, snapping my attention to him.

"You are letting him?" I ask in surprise.

Will's brow scrunches in confusion. "It's his twenty-first birthday, he is not a child? It's not up to me"

"But he is a vessel," the reply tumbles out of my mouth before I have time to think about it.

Will cocks his head to the side. "I still don't own him. I'm his uncle, nothing more. This is his house."

I look away and stare at the babbling brook. Colby is always saying that Harry and I are old-fashioned, but Colby's parents are extremely progressive, so much so that it is nearly scandalous. But now I am confused. Is Will progressive too? Is Bavaria less traditional than England? Or are Harry and I actually dinosaurs?

"Vessels are treated differently in Bavaria," says Will casually, as if he hasn't just flipping read my mind.

I cast him a wary glance. He is just perceptive, surely? He doesn't actually have mind-reading powers? Oh gosh. I have had so very many dirty thoughts about him, in his presence. I'd die of embarrassment if he turns out to be psychic.

"Are we invited to this party or are we expected to stay away like the old fogeys we are," I ask, mostly for something to say.

Will laughs. His warm, rumbling and merry laugh. Goosebumps erupt all over my flesh.

"If I'm not old, you are certainly not," he says.

"Neither of us are twenty-one," I huff.

"Ah yes. I was forgetting that you are a grand old twenty-four," Will teases.

I scowl at him. There is a whole world of difference between twenty-one and twenty-four. I don't think he is old enough to have forgotten that.

"We can attend, or we can slope off and find something more fun to do," he says.

Then he gives me a truly filthy wink. Butterflies take flight in my stomach, and my face heats. I have to snatch my gaze away again. Damn him. How does he have such an effect on me? It's most unfair.

Will sighs happily and then lies back on the blanket, resting his hands behind his head and looking up at the swaying branches of the willow tree as if he hasn't got a care in the world. His shirt has pulled up a little, and the glimpse of lightly bronzed skin is far too tantalizing. I want to lean down and lick it.

I lie down beside him, mostly so I'm not taunted by the sight of him laid out before me like some kind of offering.

The ground is not as hard as I thought it would be. This is surprisingly comfortable. And the green of the leaves against the achingly blue sky is stunning. Birds are singing and the stream is gurgling away. It really does feel as if all is well with the world. I could get used to this. Lounging around with a handsome man.

I'm sure we could be doing a lot more. If I wasn't such a coward.

I take a deep breath. Okay, Jem. Stop being such a bitch to yourself. This is all new, it's going to take some getting used to. Will is acting like a true gentleman, letting me know he is very interested, while not pushing anything. It's lovely. If a little disconcerting.

"What type of music do you like to listen to?" Will asks.

Well, he did say he wanted to get to know me. "Um, whatever is on the radio, I guess. What about you?" That seems like a nice, safe answer.

"I really like Ariana Grande."

A laugh bubbles out of me and I'm powerless to stop it. I turn my head to face Will's. "Ariana Grande?"

His brown eyes are sparkling, and his grin is huge. He is not the least bit offended. "What? I am gay, *and* European."

"What's being European got to do with anything?"

"Have you ever seen Eurovision? We love trashy pop music."

"Ariana is not trashy!" I exclaim in horror, and Will laughs in delight, and it's infectious. I'm laughing too and I can't stop. Even though he has caught me out.

"I knew you weren't as cool as you pretend to be," jibes Will.

"I am cool!" I protest. "And so is Eurovision."

"You like Eurovision?" Will looks ecstatic at the idea that I might like an over the top song contest. His expression is compelling. I'd be tempted to lie to him, just to give him what he wants to hear. Luckily I don't have to.

"I love it," I say with a soft, proud smile. Gods, I never expected to be proud to confess my love for Eurovision. What is this man doing to me?

The look of sheer joy on Will's face is worth it. I'd confess anything to see that look on him.

"It's on tonight," he says conspiratorially.

"I know," I say in a tone that I hope conveys I'm willing to go along with whatever he has in mind.

"So, let's convince Barny to turn his party into a Eurovision one," says Will with a mischievous, gleeful gleam in his eyes.

He is just so damn alluring it should be illegal. How does anyone ever process a thought whilst in his presence? My throat has suddenly gone dry, and I can't swallow.

"Sounds like a fantastic plan," I somehow manage to croak.

A beautiful, delighted smile spreads across Will's face. He really truly has to stop smiling at me like that, because every time he does, he steals another little piece of my heart.

Chapter Eleven

Will

It's hard to steal enough glances at Jem without him noticing, but I simply must try. His eyes are transfixed on the large flat-screen television and his whole face is sparkling with joy. He really does love Eurovision. I have no idea why that makes me so very happy, I only know that it does.

The sparkly, Union Jack plastic hat looks good on him. I suspect everything looks good on him, he is just that beautiful.

Jeeves wasn't able to rustle up a Bavarian hat, but he somehow managed to get hold of some bunting in the right colors. Jem laughed so much when I draped myself in it, I've made it top of my wish list to take him to bed while I'm wearing nothing but this bunting. I want to see how much that will make him laugh.

Barny and his guests are truly getting into the spirit of it too, though that probably has a lot to do with the amount of alcohol they are consuming. They seem like nice lads. All mundane, because my sister wanted to send him to a school where he would be treated like a future earl, not a vessel. I think it was a wise decision.

It's lovely to see my nephew in his element. He is clearly a daft, fun loving buffoon, but still the alpha of his friendship group.

Normally, socializing with mundanes makes me slightly uneasy. I don't know why. It's hardly as if I'm suddenly going to forget and start talking about magic, or accidentally wield some. But, nevertheless, there is always that edge that makes it impossible to fully relax. However, these young men are causing me no concern at all.

Maybe I'm getting old and more smug in my abilities. Or maybe it is because Jem is thriving in their company. To them, he is just a slightly older man. He is not a vessel or a disgrace. And Jem is glowing from it. Chatting away easily. Laughing. Returning good-natured jibes. It is like seeing his true self, and I can't tear my eyes away.

Loud cheers erupt as a song comes to an end. I have no idea what country it was. Just a vague sense that the song had a pleasant beat, and the stage was bathed in red flashing lights. Jem has stolen all of my attention. Even though I love Eurovision, and it is one of the highlights of the year for me. It would be tempting to think Jem has cast a spell on me, but he can't wield magic, he can only grow it. Any spell is purely of the infatuation variety.

"Forfeit!" yells Sam, one of Barny's guests. "You said the singer wouldn't wink at the camera, and she did!"

"She didn't wink!" protests Barny, but is soon shouted down by his friends.

I don't understand the complicated drinking game they are playing, but they seem to be having a great deal of fun with it.

"Fine!" declares Barny loudly. "I accept the forfeit!"

"Slide down the main staircase on a tray!" bellows someone gleefully.

"Challenge accepted!" says Barny proudly, as he stands up and puffs his chest out. His chin is tilted up like a statue of a noble warrior.

Then with a great deal of noise and chaos, the room empties as the boys stagger drunkenly off towards the entrance hall. I turn to Jem, in the sudden silence.

"Oh, gods!" he exclaims, as he wipes tears from his eyes from laughing. "He is going to break every bone in his body!"

I grin back at Jem. "He has to find a tray first, and then make it up the stairs. I'm pretty sure he is too drunk to do either. He will be fine."

"I hope you are right," says Jem.

"Do you want to go watch them attempt it?"

Jem shakes his head. There is a soft smile on his lips that is utterly enchanting. I am completely under his sway. If only he knew the power he holds over me.

"I need to step outside for some fresh air. It smells like a frat house in here."

"May I join you?" I ask with bated breath. It feels as if the fate of the world rests on his answer.

He nods and smiles at me, so I jump to my feet and offer him my hand. He graciously accepts it and I pull him off of the sofa. I want to pull him into my arms, and it is so hard to resist the temptation. But I do. I don't, however, release his hand. And he doesn't reclaim it. We walk hand in hand to the nearest balcony.

The fresh, cool air is wonderful. I hadn't realized quite how stuffy it was inside. This was a fabulous idea. Especially since now I'm alone on a starlit balcony with Jem.

Before us are the dark formal gardens, stretching out as far as I can see. Jem and I could be the only people in the world. It's perfect.

He leans on the stone balustrade and lets out a soft, contented sigh. A gentle night breeze ruffles his hair. We've not known each other very long, and I know we don't know each other very well, yet. But I feel so blissfully comfortable with him. His presence is soothing, familiar. I feel like I've known him forever.

The pattern of his breathing, his scent, the way he moves. It's all etched on to my soul. A part of me forever.

He turns to look at me, and I wonder what he is thinking.

"May I kiss you?" I whisper instead.

Even in the silver starlight, I can see his cheeks heat. He shakes his head, almost sadly.

"I...I don't kiss. But I'd like you to hold me."

My arms are around him, smooshing him firmly against my chest, before his words have fully left his mouth. The glittery hat falls to the floor and neither of us pay it any heed. He feels wonderful in my arms. Warm, slight and so very *Jem*. I want to hold him forever. I breathe in the scent of his hair and this feels like the happiest moment of my life.

"Your erection is digging into me," he says, muffled against my chest.

I loosen my hold on him, just a fraction. "Oh, sorry."

He chuckles. "It's fine. I'll take it as a compliment."

Another smile stretches across my face. I grin so much when around him, my face aches. It is truly wonderful. Jem is a blessing.

My hands slide down his back, to the very top of his incredible ass.

"Is this okay?" I whisper.

"Hmm hm," he murmurs.

I allow my hands to lower until I'm cupping his ass cheeks. Now I'm caressing and jiggling them. Pert and juicy. Utterly perfect. Just like Jem.

He gives me a soft moan and presses himself closer to me. Now I can feel his erection and nothing has ever made me prouder. A few more minutes of this, and then I will suggest that we take this upstairs.

An immense wave of magic blasts through the air. It feels like an atom bomb detonating a few feet away. The shock waves ripple through me. Jem and I step apart and stare at each other in shocked confusion. The cold realization strikes. That was a vessel being tapped.

I don't know how much Jem felt, or what exactly it felt like to him, but as I open my mouth, he whispers "Barny," in horror.

He has figured it out too.

Chapter Twelve

Will

As one, we turn and race inside. Running towards the epicenter of the magic blast. We reach the library door the same time that Jeeves does, and all three of us pile in.

Barny is sprawled face down over a chaise lounge. His trousers are around his ankles. He is alone, there is no one else in sight. Jem hurries over to him and pulls his trousers up. Then he brushes Barny's blond hair away from his face. My nephew mumbles something incoherent. His blue eyes are blurry and unfocused. He is completely out of it, far more so than the last time I saw him. Has he been drugged?

Jem glares at me, his aquamarine eyes bright and fierce. "Go get the bastard!"

I turn to Jeeves, just in time to see a flash of flames and fury in his abyss dark eyes, then he is gone.

"I don't think Jeeves needs my help," I say dumbfoundedly.

"Then help me carry Barny to his room," orders Jem.

His sharp tone snaps me out of my stupor, and I stride forward. We get Barny standing and Jem puts his arm over his shoulders, in an effort to hold Barny steady, but Barny is swaying so much, it's clear that will not work, even if I take the other side. So I scoop my nephew up into a bridal carry and start striding towards his rooms. Jem hurries along beside me.

We reach Barny's bedchamber and I gently place my nephew down on his bed. Then I'm frozen in inaction once more. I'm too shocked to think, let alone be capable of deciding what to do.

Jem however, is a flurry of activity. He finds a clean nightgown. He gets a warm wet cloth, and he deftly strips Barny, cleans him up and dresses him in the nightgown. All while I stand here, as useful as a statue.

Jeeves walks in and the anger radiating off of him is truly terrifying. It feels like a dark, insidious cloud filling the room.

"Did you catch him?" I say.

The butler gives one sharp nod. "One of his guests. A stupid mundane with just enough residual magic to tap Barny."

I don't know what to think about that. I guess it's good that it wasn't a mage planning on claiming Barny as his vessel. But on the other hand, the thought that my nephew's life has been ruined because of some drunken, barely-past-teen horniness, is devastating.

I look at Jeeves and nearly ask what he has done to the perpetrator, but one look into his dark inhuman eyes, and I really don't want to know.

"I can use dark magic to conceal the fact that Barny has been tapped," says Jeeves, almost calmly. "The only people who would know, are those who are in the room presently. We would need to take a vow of silence."

"Agreed!" says Jem passionately, without a moment's hesitation. Then his dazzling eyes fix on me expectantly.

I swallow. Dark magic? Vows of silence? Somehow I'm not the least bit surprised that Jeeves is a practitioner of the dark arts, but I'm not sure I want to be complacent in it. No magic of the light can conceal that a vessel has been tapped. I had no idea that dark magic could do such a thing. It's unsettling as hell, but it would solve a lot of problems. It could make it as if this awful night had never happened. Barny could go on with his life.

Or I could renounce Jeeves as a practitioner and have him thrown out of Barny's service. I could report him to the mage council and have him arrested. The butler has to know all this. He is choosing to expose himself, for Barny's sake.

My gaze falls on the tousled blond hair of my nephew. He is sleeping. But his newly freed magic is pulsing, open, vulnerable. People are going to want to take it. Now more than ever. Nevermind the shame he will face in society as tapped and unwed. He will be disgraced, like Jem.

Unless he can find someone to marry him. He is soon to be an earl, so that is entirely still possible. But it will probably be an unsavory person. Not one that cares for him. One that just wants his title and his magic. And to take advantage of the unfortunate situation.

It's an awful predicament. One that merely staying silent and concealing won't solve. The problem is far deeper than that.

"But he has been tapped," I say. "He will need emptying regularly now, by someone discreet, a magic user who can also be sworn to secrecy."

"Indeed, Your Highness," says Jeeves, insidiously.

I shiver. My nephew being emptied by his creepy butler? I suppose it's not a terrible solution. Certainly no one will suspect a thing when they are alone together. But it still makes me uncomfortable.

"I agree to the silence part. The...er...emptying will need to be agreed by Barny when he is awake."

"Of course, Your Highness," agrees Jeeves smoothly.

If he is insulted by my suggestion that he might not seek Barny's consent, he is not showing it. I'm very glad of that. Jeeves is a deeply terrifying man.

"Do you need any assistance with the casting?" I ask uneasily. I want as little part of dark magic as possible.

"No thank you, Your Highness. However, please be aware the spell will work most effectively, if the situation is never spoken aloud," says Jeeves. He fixes me with a stern stare. "Even when you and Mr. Cambell are alone together."

Jem blushes and mumbles his understanding and agreement.

"Understood," I say. "We will leave you to it."

"Thank you, Your Highness," says Jeeves and he walks us to the door. As soon as we step into the hallway, the door shuts firmly. Almost in our faces. The sound has a ring of finality to it. I hope I have made the right decision.

Jem is staring at me. We can't talk about what just happened. Not now, not ever. Whatever happens between us, I know Jem will never breathe a word. My trust in him is absolute. And it is not merely because Jem has had to live the consequences of being disgraced. Jem is an honorable person. He will always do the right thing. I can feel that in my soul.

"I need a drink," I say.

"Me too," agrees Jem.

We walk towards our rooms. Getting blindly drunk sounds like the best possible end to this night.

Chapter Thirteen

Jem

Sunlight is piercing my eyelids and invading my skull. My mouth is dry and tastes like a sewer. Slowly I become aware of my surroundings, and I am sprawled face down on a bed. On top of the covers, with all my clothes on.

Thoughts of poor Barny start to crowd my mind. I push them aside. I can't ever talk about it. And everything has been resolved as best as it can be, so there is no point in dwelling on it. Besides, my current suffering is consuming all of my attention.

Blearily, I open my eyes and find that Will is lying next to me, in a similar disheveled state as me. We are in his room, and I guess we passed out after drinking far too much. A steady pounding starts in my head. I groan.

Will's eyes open, and he stares at me with a slightly unfocussed gaze for a moment. "Did we...?"

We are in his bed, so it is a reasonable question. But we are both fully dressed and my ass doesn't feel used at all. I'm sure I'd feel it. As well as remember it.

I shake my head and instantly regret the movement, almost as much as I regret the fact that nothing happened.

Will huffs out a sigh of relief, and indignation coils through me instantly, but then he smiles.

"Only because I don't want to take advantage of you."

I give him a scowl. That is slightly mollifying, I guess. Though, truthfully, I want Will to take advantage of me. Very much so. It would save me from having to find the courage to make the first move.

"Do you want me to get rid of that hangover for you?" he asks.

"Do bears shit in the woods?" I snap.

Will laughs as if my words are utterly hilarious. He is acting like he thinks I should be a stand-up comedian.

"You might be one of those people who believes they should suffer the consequences of their actions," he says.

"Fuck that!" I grumble. Even though in other areas of my life, that is exactly what I believe.

Will smiles at me, leans over and places two fingers on my forehead. His magic tingles through me and then my headache vanishes. Followed swiftly by my grogginess. This is incredible.

He does the spell on himself and sighs in relief.

"I need to get more mage friends," I say.

Will grins, but I think that was a flash of jealousy I saw in his eyes. The thought of that makes me shiver in a delightful way. Will getting possessive over me? I think I could live with that. It would be a dream come true to mean that much to someone, especially him.

My stomach rumbles loudly. "Oh, gods! I'm starving!" I exclaim as a wave of intense hunger washes over me.

"Sorry! It's a side effect of the spell. I should have told you," says Will, just as his own stomach gurgles.

I giggle. An honest to god giggle. I've never made such a sound in my entire life. I wasn't aware that I could. I stare at Will in mortification but he just has a soppy look on his face, as if he thought my giggle was endearing or something. This man is impossible.

"Shower, then downstairs for breakfast?" I suggest.

Will's eyes gleam. "Sounds like a splendid plan."

"Separate showers," I clarify, then immediately wonder why I said that. Showering with Will would be amazing. I can just picture his wet, naked and soapy body. I can imagine him running his hands all over me.

Hastily, I jump out of bed, before he has a chance to see my sudden and intense arousal.

"I know," says Will with a cheeky grin that leaves me wondering what exactly it is that he knows.

I mumble something incoherent and slip through the interconnecting door to my own rooms. I want to have the quickest shower in the history of the universe, so I can race down to the breakfast room and be back in Will's company as soon as possible.

Oh my, I really do have it bad.

After a super quick wash and throwing on some clean clothes, I hurry downstairs to find that Will has somehow beaten me to it, and to my surprise, Barny is also seated at the breakfast table.

I do a double and then a triple take. He is sitting there, as clear as day, but my senses are telling me that his magic is untapped. He seems exactly like a virgin vessel.

My gaze flicks to Jeeves who is standing unobtrusively in the corner. The butler gives me a slight nod of acknowledgment. Damn, his magic casting is top-notch.

I stare at Barny again. Apart from some dark circles under his eyes, he looks none the worse for wear, but I know all too well how appearances can be deceptive.

"Good morning Barny. How are you feeling?" I say. I hope that counts as not talking about it. It's vague enough that it could mean anything. We can pretend to talk about him getting too drunk and needing to be carried to his rooms.

Barny bites his bottom lip and looks down. "I feel fine, thank you. I don't remember much about last night. I'm sorry for the inconvenience."

"Barny, you are not an inconvenience," I say as I sit down next to Will.

"Thank you," mumbles Barny while staring at his yogurt.

Poor kid. My heart bleeds for him, it really does. I hope he has the strength to get through this.

Will smiles warmly at me and pours me a coffee. He looks far finer than any man who has had the night he has should. Even with magic hangover cures. He smells damn good too. That fresh from the shower man scent that is impossible to resist. It's going to take all my willpower not to climb onto his lap.

"I was thinking that I'd like to find a husband," says Barny. "Everyone says vessels are happier with a mage."

"Are you sure that is what you want?" asks Will.

Barny nods. "It seems like the most sensible course of action. I'd be grateful if you could let it be known that I'm open to be courted."

It does make a whole heap of sense. Attend a lot of society events. Find an amenable mage from a good family. Trick him into thinking Barny is still a virgin. Then after the wedding night, this disaster will be well and truly solved.

"Of course," agrees Will.

A flash of jealousy surges through me. I wish Harry had been so supportive. But he had been so young, our parents had just died, and he had been surrounded by assholes. It's not his fault that he hadn't known any better.

And it's not as if we had a Jeeves to hide my mistake. Or as Colby insists, my abuse. A wave of gloom washes over me as I think about how very different my life might have been.

Under the table, Will gives my knee a reassuring squeeze. The bloody bastard better not be psychic. I'll kill him for not confessing that fact to me. Hopefully, I'm just easy to read. Which is nearly as bad, though not quite.

"How about a game of tennis after breakfast?" says Will.

"Tennis?" I repeat in surprise.

"I reckon I can thrash you!" teases Will warmly.

"You're on," I grin back.

I'm not bad at tennis, and the distraction will be good, which is probably Will's intention. And to be honest, any excuse to spend time with Will is fine by me.

Any excuse at all.

Chapter Fourteen

Will

Those aren't tennis shorts Jem is wearing. They are far tighter and far shorter. And I am not complaining. At all. He looks stunning. So much so that it is throwing me off of my game. I'm pretty sure the only reason I'm able to play at all is that when Jem reaches up to hit the ball, his loose top flows up and I get a flash of his belly button ring. It's red today. Like the night we met, and it's giving my cock all sorts of ideas.

"I need a break!" pleads Jem, and I am more than happy to oblige.

He drops his racket and heads over to the drinking fountain in the corner of the court. I trail after him. He bends over to drink right in front of me and I am presented with the sight of his wonderful ass. I quickly adjust myself, while he is not looking.

He stands up and grins at me. Water droplets are running down his chin and he uses the back of his hand to wipe them away. His cheeks are flushed and he is breathing heavily. I know it's exertion from playing tennis, but it sure is reminding me of sex.

I shuffle forward, bend over and take a drink too. It's a great way to hide the growing bulge in my shorts. But I can't slurp at this cool water forever.

Jem opens the gate in the chain-link fence that stops balls flying everywhere. He walks a few steps on the grass, then flops down on his back in the shade of a tree. His arms are above his head and he is still panting. Is he trying to seduce me on purpose? I hope so.

Helplessly, I walk up to him. The pull of his allure is stronger than the gravity of a black hole. There is no choice. I can only remain in his orbit. Standing here, staring down and drinking in the sight of him.

His midriff is exposed, and his ruby red piercing is winking at me.

"What are you thinking?" he asks as he looks up at me. His eyes are sparkling like gems. He truly has the right name. He is my precious Jem.

I swallow. "I'm wondering how hard it will be to peel those shorts off of you."

Jem gives me a truly sultry smile. "How about we find out?"

He is feeling horny too? This is the best news I have ever heard. My cock throbs. My heart flutters. There is no one else in the gardens. I managed to convince Mark that I don't need a bodyguard when I'm with Jem. We are all alone. This spot can't even be seen from the house.

I throw myself down on top of him. He laughs. He told me last night that he doesn't kiss, so I attack his neck instead. Licking, nibbling, devouring. He makes a soft noise that sets my soul alight. He wraps his arms around me and I'm in heaven. Finally.

I place my hand on his stomach and slide it up under his top, to a pierced nipple. I tweak it between my fingers. Jem gasps and his back arches off of the grass. So I lower my head and use my lips to toy with his other nipple. Soon he is a writhing, squirming undone mess before me. It is glorious.

I release one nipple, so that I can pop the button on his shorts. I slide down the fly and his cock bounces out, free in the summer air. I knew he couldn't have been wearing underwear.

I give his cock a light, teasing stroke with my fingers and Jem whines and bucks into my hand. I kiss my way down his stomach. Then I swallow him whole. Jem's hips lift up off the grass and he wails.

Chuckling I move my hands to his hips so I can hold him down while I ravish his cock. He thrashes and keens as I take him all the way into my throat. I swallow around him and the carnal, depraved noise he makes is food for my soul.

I fumble down to my fly and free my constrained cock. I moan around Jem's cock from the sheer relief.

"S...Stop!" he stutters.

I pull off of him with a wet plop. He groans.

"Okay?" I ask.

His eyes are closed, his cheeks red and his breaths fast and frantic. He looks like a painting of pleasure and I couldn't be prouder.

He nods against the green grass under his head. "I want to cum with you inside me."

My vision whites out and for a moment I think I've peaked just from hearing those words on his lips.

"Stay right there!" I yell as I jump to my feet and sprint over to my kit bag.

Sprinting with my full cock bouncing free and naked in the sunshine feels strangely good.

I yank the zip on the bag so hard it pings off, but I don't care, it's open. I quickly find what I'm looking for and I run back to Jem. His eyes are open and he is staring at my hand.

"You packed lube in your tennis bag?" he asks, with an incredulous look on his face.

"I was a boy scout," I grin. "The motto was, always be prepared."

Jem's eyes widen and then he laughs, a full, belly deep laugh. "You bastard! Now I'm going to think of butt sex every time I hear that saying!"

I puff my chest out, "Good!"

He laughs some more and I flop down beside him.

"We might need to use it all to get those shorts off," I say wryly.

He huffs at me and rolls his eyes. "They aren't that tight."

He lifts his hips off of the ground once more and starts pushing them down. They roll as they go and he stops when they are mid thigh.

"Okay, maybe they are," he says.

I laugh and drop the lube on the grass, so both of my hands are free to yank on his shorts. It's hard work but with swearing and giggling and working together, we manage it.

As soon as he is free, I can't resist sucking on his cock again. He gasps and moans. His fingers card through my hair. His legs spread wide in invitation. I fumble for the lube bottle and manage to squirt a generous glob right on his taint. I guide it down to his hole, swirl it around, and then slowly ease my finger into his tight, silken heat. We groan at the same time. He feels so good. My cock throbs impatiently. I want my cock to be enveloped by Jem and feeling what my finger is feeling.

I add another finger, even though I'm worried it might be too soon, but Jem takes it well and his deep groan tells me he is enjoying it.

I crook my fingers and search for his prostate. He bucks and swears. I chuckle. I think I've found it. I stroke it again and he yells. But he wants to cum with me inside him. I want that too. More than I've ever wanted anything. Right now I feel as if I need that more than I need oxygen.

I scissor my fingers, stretching and opening him up for me. When I give him my cock, I want it to feel only good. I don't want there to be any pain, only bliss.

He lets out a cry that I feel in my bones. My most primal self recognizes it. If I don't hurry up, I'm going to miss my chance. Hurriedly, I pull out my fingers. Jem whines. I line up my aching cock and nudge it against his entrance. Jem gasps and throws his head back. This beautiful man is ready for me. He wants to take me. He needs me to fill him and rock his world.

Slowly, I slide into him. The feel of his silken heat engulfing my hard cock is exquisite. The way his breath is hitching and his muscles are trembling from the pleasure I am giving him, is filling my soul with joy. I could worship Jem forever. The sounds of lust I'm coaxing from him could be my prayers, my absolution.

His body opens up for me and I sink all the way in. He is undulating with need, so I rock my hips. The slide of my cock inside of him causes delicious frisson to shoot along my cock and up into my body where it dances along every nerve in my body. Pleasure, lust and desire consumes me until I am nothing but euphoria.

We find a rhythm, I push, he lifts. Our bodies dance together, seeking the ultimate joy. Pure ecstasy is running through my veins. I'm panting, I'm sweating. My flesh is slapping against his. At this moment I am closer to a primal beast than I have ever been, yet I am also the most enlightened.

I roll us so I'm lying on my back on the grass and Jem is above me. Straddling me and riding me. He gasps and his eyes grow huge. This position opens him up even more and I sink in even deeper. Penetrating him fully. My hands on his hips help him rise up and slam back down. Once, twice. On the third time, his eyes roll back. His body spasms. His hole clenches tight around my cock and he peaks beautifully, with a long, low keening cry.

His cock spurts and spurts and then mine is doing the same, buried deep inside him. My orgasm rushes through me, scattering me with the force of an exploding star.

Magic flows out of Jem. It pours into me. Rich and potent. It fills every part of my being. It's not as intense as when he was ripe, but it's still incredible. It feels as if I have enough power now to cast any spell known to mankind. I feel invincible. It is a hell of a buzz.

On top of me, Jem slumps. His head tips forward. His body starts to shudder. Still inside him, I sit up and wrap my arms around him. He leans into my embrace. I hold him and I don't know how I am ever going to let him go.

Chapter Fifteen

Will

I run into Jem's bedchamber in such a panic, that I don't even knock.

"Jeeves said you were packing!" I exclaim unnecessarily.

There was no need to say that, when right before me I can see the half filled open suitcase on the bed and Jem putting things into it.

Jem gives me a soft smile. "I was going to come talk to you."

"What's wrong! What did I do? I'm so sorry!" I burble in sheer panic.

I thought our time by the tennis courts earlier today was earth moving for him too. Have I pushed him too far, too soon? Am I being too intense?

Jem shakes his head at me, as if he thinks I'm being daft. "Nothing is wrong, I just need to go home for two nights."

"Why?" I ask weakly, even though it's prying and rude. I need to know. I need to believe Jem's assertion that I haven't fucked up and made him run away. My heart is pounding with urgency.

He pauses in his packing and looks calmly right at me. Meeting my gaze steadily and letting me see the truth of his words. "I have an exam and apparently hooking up with a hot guy is not an extenuating circumstance that allows me to postpone it."

I blink for a few moments as my mind processes what Jem just said. Of all the things he could have told me, this wasn't even on my list. And he said I was a hot guy. But that last piece of information is sadly something I need to put away for now. I can preen about it later. Right now there are far more important things to focus on.

"Did you tell them I was a prince?" I hear myself say.

Jem laughs. "I should have tried that."

"You are at university?" I ask, as my mind slowly works through this new information.

He flushes, drops my gaze and resumes packing. "Just the Open University, it's distance learning. Apart from exams."

"It's still a proper university," I say.

Jem shrugs. "It's just something to pass the time. Since my brother got married and his consort has taken over running the house, I have even more spare hours than ever."

He says it so calmly, so matter of fact, when in reality it's an awful insight to his life. It sounds lonely, empty. He is expected just to lie around until he is ripe, and then the mage council chooses which mage gets his magic.

And his body. My hands ball into fists by my sides.

Jem shoots me a worried look. "I really want to start a masters in September and this last module I am doing has been discontinued, so if I skip the exam, I'll have to do a whole new module before I can graduate."

"Of course you should go!" I exclaim. He shouldn't upend his education for me. The thought shouldn't even cross his mind.

"Maybe I should stay?" says Jem, and he bites his bottom lip. "It is just a hobby. This is my third degree. It's not important."

"You have three degrees?" I exclaim.

"Two at the moment," he insists.

"That is incredible!"

Jem shakes his head, "It's really not. It's just something to do in the evening instead of scrolling on my phone. I've been doing it for years, but now I have even more time, I want to try a masters."

This man is impossible. How can I get him to not be so dismissive of his accomplishments? He is incredible, and he needs to see that.

"What are you studying?" I ask. Perhaps if I get him to talk enthusiastically about his studies, I can encourage him to see how wonderful he is.

Jem winces and seems to brace himself for ridicule. "Physics," he mumbles while staring at the half folded tee shirt in his hands.

"Oh wow, that's amazing!" I exclaim in awe. That truly is an impressive subject. "What are your other degrees in?"

"Advanced mathematics and Biomedical sciences," he all but whispers.

"Flipping heck, Jem, you are a genius!"

He looks up at me in surprise, and it hurts. What was he expecting? What has he been taught to expect? To be told that he is silly and that vessels don't have the brains for such subjects? That they should concentrate on pleasing their husbands and keeping the house in order? Or even worse bigotry, such as, vessels are only good for giving their magic to their master. I hate all that old-fashioned nonsense with a passion.

But Jem doesn't need a lecture from me. He needs support and encouragement. I stride up to him and wrap my arms around him.

"I'm courting a genius!" I puff in pride.

He goes rigid in my arms. Stiffer than a statue. Then he steps back, breaking out of my embrace. His dazzling eyes are burning fiercely.

"You are not courting me!" he snaps.

I stare at him. My mouth opens and shuts a few times. "I...er thought I was?" I'm so confused. What is happening right now?

Jem's eyes narrow. "You are hardly going to propose, are you?"

Now I'm completely and utterly lost. "Why wouldn't I?" I hedge cautiously. I have no wish to make him even more angry.

"Because I'm not exactly suitable, am I!" bites Jem ferociously.

"Why on earth not? You're a vessel and the brother of a duke. That sounds entirely and extremely suitable to me."

"I am disgraced! And don't pretend you don't care about that. You would never invite a respectable vessel to spend the summer with you, unchaperoned, in adjoining bedchambers."

I feel my cheeks heat as shame floods through me. He is right. I wouldn't. No vessels' family would let me, for a start. But I don't think any less of Jem. Not at all. I assumed he was carefree and rebellious and didn't give a shit about all of that. It was intoxicating.

But now, as I stare back at Jem and see the tears brimming in his eyes, I'm filled with gut wrenching horror. Jem does care. Very much so. He thinks I brought him here as just a bit of fun. Because he believes he is not worth any more than that.

My heart feels like it is breaking. I don't know how to fix this. All the time he has been here, this is what he believed? That he was nothing more to me than saucy entertainment? This is a miscommunication of epic proportions. I should have understood the depths of this when he freaked out on our first night here.

I thought I had grasped it then, but I hadn't really. I'd merely seen the tip of the iceberg and I didn't care to look any deeper, because a large part of me did just want to have a fun and dirty summer with this incredible and enticing young man.

"I'm so sorry, Jem," I say softly.

There are no words for everything I need to say. At least none that I can catch and form coherently right now. I can only hope he can see some of my meaning in my body language and tone.

"It's fine," he sniffs as he resumes packing. But it is far from fine.

I stand silently and watch him move around the room. It's as if a light has been switched on in my mind and suddenly I can see through my dumb, horny fog.

I see him now. I finally understand. He has been shunned by society. Regulated to a thing that is passed around and used for his magic. In response, Jem has held his head up high, gone 'fuck you,' and given them attitude in return. Dressed flamboyantly. Played the part of a sex toy to the max. Embraced the role he was assigned.

But really, he wants it all to stop. He yearns to be loved, cherished. Safe.

He doesn't want to be scorned. He wants to be accepted. Respected. Underneath his tough exterior, he is so very vulnerable. A little lost. A whole lot frightened.

All these years he has been so brave, so utterly alone.

Then I came along and acted like he was a delightful sexy toy to play with. Something to amuse me for the summer. Just another jerk in his life. Another asshole.

I haven't made it clear enough that I really like him. I haven't shown him that I'm different. Oh gods, I hope I am different. I can't bear the thought that I'm merely the latest man to take advantage of him and his unfortunate situation.

"I really like you, Jem," I say earnestly.

He glances up from his packing just long enough to give me a thoroughly disparaging look. It feels like my soul is withering. But Jem is right. This is not something a few mere words is going to put right. I'm going to have to earn Jem's trust with actions and time.

I step up behind him and slip my arms around his waist. He freezes.

"I'm sorry Jem, I've been an ass. Please let me make it up to you."

He relaxes a little in my embrace. But it is not enough. It is nowhere near enough.

"I don't want you to leave on an argument," I plead.

Jem sighs and sags back against me. "Okay," he sighs.

And that is going to have to do. For now.

Chapter Sixteen

Will

I'm staring at this newspaper but the words are just not going in. Jem has been gone for one entire night and I can't stand it. His exam is starting soon, so I can't even call or text him. All I can do is pine like a lost puppy.

I bring the coffee cup to my lips. Ugh, it's cold. How long have I been sitting here at the breakfast table?

"Let me pour you a fresh coffee, Your Highness," says Jeeves smoothly.

He efficiently removes my neglected cup and replaces it with a steaming one that smells fantastic.

"Thank you, Jeeves."

The butler bows his head and moves discreetly back.

"Jeeves, may I ask you something?"

"Of course, Your Highness."

My stomach is in knots, and my heart is racing. I've gone back and forth over this and I feel vile for doing it. But I have to know.

What did Jem do that he now regrets so much? I'm not being nosy, I swear I'm not. At least I bloody well hope so. I hope what I am telling myself is true. That I want to understand Jem. I want to put his puzzle pieces together.

And I definitely don't want to do anything that might ignite bad memories for him.

I don't want him to regret me.

"How was Jem disgraced?"

Staff always know these things, and even if they didn't, Jeeves would know. I have a feeling Jeeves knows everything. Including the very secrets of how the universe works.

The butler serenely steps into my line of sight, so I don't have to crick my neck. His dark eyes glint at me in silence for a moment.

"The gossips say he seduced his trainer."

My body freezes. My lungs stutter to a halt. What ludicrous nonsense is this? The man who was supposed to teach Jem the sixty-nine positions a vessel may assume for his master, would have been a professional. An adult. Jem would have been young, if his family followed the English tradition.

His trainer was supposed to teach him positions and how to draw summoning circles as well as how to do basic incantations. Very old-fashioned and barbaric trainers use dildos too, as they claim to 'teach vessels how to take a cock.'

But even if that vileness takes place, vessels remain a virgin. It's imperative. No teenager would have the ability to make a professional forget that.

I try to swallow but my throat has seized up.

Jem was abused. Jem was abused and blamed for it. Jem was abused and blamed for it and is still being punished for it.

The coffee cup explodes into a million pieces, sending scalding hot coffee up in the air like a fountain. I manage to move out of the way for its descent and the dark liquid spreads all over the crisp white linen tablecloth. I stare aghast at the destruction I have wrought.

"Oh, please forgive me, Jeeves!" I exclaim.

Such a loss of control is shocking. I'm absolutely mortified.

"There is nothing to forgive, Your Highness. The topic of conversation is emotive."

Jeeves calmly steps forward and begins dealing with the mess I inadvertently made. I mumble a further apology and hastily retreat to my rooms. I need to regain control and pull myself together.

As I race down the hallway, I am assaulted by images. Jem lying against the snow-white sheets in the penthouse and tensing at my approach. Jem fumbling with his buttons on his first night here because he assumed I was going to demand sex.

My memories loop back to the night we met and how on edge Jem had been. Then they skip forward to his first dinner here and how miserable and nervous he had seemed. I think I know the reason now. Because he thought I was going to take him upstairs and ravish him.

Oh, my gods. I've been such an idiot. Jem is not disgruntled at being given to a different mage every time he is ripe. He doesn't dislike the situation. He is scared. He is frightened.

He was abused when he was a teenager. Taken advantage of. Forced. And it has been happening every single month since.

I've reached my rooms, and the chandelier is shaking. I take a deep breath. I need to calm down. I need to keep my magic under control.

Am I just the latest man to take advantage of Jem? The noise that comes out of me sounds like an animal in distress. I guess that is fitting. It's more or less what I am.

I throw myself down on my bed and try to think. Try to recall and analyze my every moment with Jem. Everything I said. Everything I've done. Every way I have treated him.

I groan. Okay. I'm not proud of that first night, but since then I think I've treated him well. Images of making love by the tennis court play in my mind's eye. It was making love and not sex, wasn't it? Jem was into it? It wasn't something that he thought he had to do?

I see him framed by the leaves of the tree, his dazzling eyes looking down at me as he rode my cock. A sigh of relief escapes me. I'm pretty sure that was all good. I think Jem likes me, wants me. I really want to believe he feels safe with me.

Is that why he got so angry and upset over my courting comment? Because he wants to be courted by me, but thinks it isn't possible? Please don't tell me that Jem believes he is trash. He seems too strong and far too defiant to take how he has been treated to heart. But emotions, feelings, beliefs are complex and rarely rational. One can know a thing, but not truly believe it.

I sigh despondently. Poor Jem. He doesn't deserve this, nobody does. How could he have suffered all this and still be such a lovely person? He is funny, clever, dazzling and fierce. I would have been lost without him during Barney's disaster.

Jem is the most incredible man I have ever met.

The truth of those words take a while to sink into me. Then they toll like a bell, sending reverberations through my soul and shaking everything into place. Suddenly, everything is blindingly crystal clear.

Oh, my. I'm such an idiot.

The strength of my anger, and the intensity of my feeling of protectiveness at hearing his awful history. It's bloody obvious.

I love Jem.

I don't want a summer fling. I want him by my side forever. I want to spend my life with him.

Jem is the one.

Chapter Seventeen

Jem

My head is pounding. I feel like I'm going to vomit. Thank heavens I didn't feel like this during the exam. My magic was kind enough to wait until I got home to start to brim over. Not that it has any sort of consciousness or ability to plan, but it has always felt so 'other,' so separate to me, that I always fall into the trap of thinking of it as a separate entity.

Now it is building within me. Restless and brooding.

I hate this feeling and I'd much rather try to deal with it in the privacy of my own home. For as long as I can.

"Jem? Jem, How was the exam?" calls Colby as he lets himself into my sitting room.

I don't move from my undignified sprawl on the sofa. I'm not sure I could, even if I wanted to. I feel pathetically grateful that Colby is here. His company is strangely soothing. I have no idea why I am being such a baby.

"It was fine," I rasp.

Colby stops and stands there, staring at me for a moment. He does nothing but blink.

"You're ripe," he says eventually.

I hate the way my cheeks are heating but there is not a thing I can do about it. "Well, yes. My cycle is bound to be all over the place," I stammer. Great. Now I've given my brother-in-law the impression that Will and I have been at it like rabbits.

Colby's eyes light up with glee. "You lucky bastard!"

"When is Harry coming back from Japan?" I say in an effort to distract Colby and change the topic of conversation.

"Day after tomorrow," answers Colby dismissively. "You better hurry back to your prince!"

I groan. Will is not my prince. He is not my anything. Despite how very much I wish it were otherwise.

Time to put on my best 'I don't give a shit about anything expression.' It feels like putting on a well-worn pair of shoes. Comforting and familiar. Everything molded to the shape of me. I can do this. I've always done this.

"No, no. Rocester Hall is miles away. I've notified the Council and a car will be here soon."

Colby's eyes grow huge and he staggers into a chair. "Why would you do that!" he gasps in horror. "I thought you liked Will?"

I shrug. "He's okay, but he is not here. Besides, I have to notify the Council when I'm ripe."

Wow, I'm good at this. I really do sound like I don't care and that this is just a mild inconvenience. Nobody could tell that I'm scared. Scared of disobeying the Council. Scared of obeying them. Scared of admitting my feelings for Will.

Tom walks briskly in. "Your car has arrived, Mr. Cambell."

Adrenaline spikes through me. Fantastic. Now I have to hide my shaking from Colby. I swiftly roll to my feet.

"Don't go," says Colby. "Call Will."

I shake my head. If I open my mouth, I might sob instead. I walk determinedly towards the door. Focusing on just putting one foot in front of the other.

"Jem! You are being an idiot!" calls Colby.

He is probably right. But it is far too late now.

This ritual room is nasty. It's deep in the basement of the house. All damp and dark and claustrophobic.

I've not met this mage before. He is older, with silver streaks in his hair. The slightly crazed, glassy look in his eyes of someone who spends all their time alone and wrapped up in their studies.

My guess is that he has recently made some sort of breakthrough and petitioned the Council for the use of a vessel, to gain some extra magic in order to complete the next step.

Not that it matters. I've been sent here, and that is that. It will all be over soon enough.

The chalk breaks and I swear. The mage ordered me to draw a specific casting circle, but between the uneven concrete floor and the shit piece of chalk he has given me, it's proving difficult.

He seems harmless enough, but I still want it done before he returns. I'm almost looking forward to hearing his footsteps on the creaky stairs, because at least then I won't be down here alone.

My hands pick up the pace of drawing the required symbols on the floor. The piece of chalk is smaller now, but just about still functionable.

There. All done. I brush off my hands and admire my handiwork. Just in time, because I can hear his footsteps approaching. I look up and give the mage my best flirtatious smile. People always treat you better when they like you. But he just frowns slightly. Perfect. It's either men he doesn't like or sex in general. Either way, I'm not going to be able to win him over. To him I'm just a tool. Something he can extract magic from.

"Ka-ra-nei," he says.

Well, fuck him then. My hands shake as I start to undress. He wants me on my knees, head on the floor, ass in the air. Not the most dignified position, and one I swear is not necessary for the spell he is attempting. But it's not like I have a choice.

As I strip, I feel myself close down. My mind is starting to drift away. Somewhere safe. Somewhere far more pleasant. I'll come back to my body when this is all over.

If only I can stop thinking about Will. I don't want to think of him while I am in this horrid place. It feels like tainting my happy memories, as if the darkness here can seep into Will via my thoughts.

But as much as I want to protect Will. I can't keep him out of my mind. My body is craving his. I'm longing for him to be the one to empty me. I want his kindness. His passion. His dorky sense of humor. I want all of him and I wish he was here.

I should have called him. I'm such an idiot. He is a prince, I'm sure he could have told the Council to go fuck themselves. There was no need for me to be such a coward.

But I wasn't just being a coward was I? I was doing a Jem and freaking out at the merest hint of happiness, and flying into sabotage and self-destruct mode. What better way to do that than to show Will what I really am? Make him be disgusted with me.

I take in a deep breath. What the hell was I thinking? Why couldn't I allow myself to enjoy one lousy summer? Will is not going to want me back at Rocester Hall after this.

I get into position on the floor. The mage walks around me, chanting, preparing his spell. I shiver. It's even colder down here when you are naked.

My magic is swirling through me, swelling and throbbing within me. Desperate for release. It wants to be free. It wants to escape my useless body that cannot wield it. It will force my body to enjoy whatever mage possesses it. I know this. I know I have no choice, no power here. So why the hell do I feel like I'm betraying Will?

I bite my bottom lip in an effort to stifle a sob. I don't want to be here. I've never regretted anything more. This is the worst mistake of my life.

Okay, deep breath. Calm the fuck down, Jem. Will was only ever going to be an interlude to your life. Once the summer is over, he is going back to Bavaria and you are never going to see him again. You've fucked up by making everything crash down sooner than it was due to, but it is hardly the end of the world. This is your real life. You can't forget that.

Alright, talking to myself isn't a great indication of sanity, but I think it is helping. I want to be calm by the time the mage steps into the circle and joins me. I can do this. I always do this.

This is my life.

Chapter Eighteen

Will

As the portal forms, I can see Jem and the basement before anyone in there is aware of my spying. Jem is naked on the floor, in the middle of a casting circle. His ass is up and the red ruby of his butt plug is winking at me.

The sight releases a tsunami of emotions within me. None of them I can name. All of them intense and as fierce as a forest fire.

I step through the portal and leave it open behind me. Lord Smythe draws himself up to his full height and bellows at me. His face all contorted and inhuman looking in the pulsing purple light of my portal.

"What is the meaning of this!"

I open my mouth to explain, I have words prepared, but my fist flies up and smashes into Lord Smythe's face instead, sending him cartwheeling backwards to the dusty floor.

I'm sure I should feel bad. Technically, Lord Smythe has done nothing wrong. By the look of things, he hasn't even laid a finger on my Jem.

But I'm beyond caring. There is not the slightest slither of remorse within me. There is only a dark satisfaction. Hitting the man who dared to take Jem feels right.

I turn to Jem. He hasn't moved. Hasn't lifted up his head to see what all the commotion is about. As I step closer, I can see he is trembling. My white hot rage intensifies.

Somehow, I manage to whip off my jacket, scoop Jem up into my arms and cover him with it. Then I step back through the portal, into my room at Rocester Hall. Behind me, the portal winks out of existence.

The sudden return to light, normalcy and safety, is a little disorientating. But so very welcome. Though I can't breathe a sigh of relief, not yet. I need to know that Jem is okay.

Jem blinks up at me. His eyes are huge, his face is pale. It's clear he is struggling to process the abrupt change in his situation. Which is a very understandable reaction.

"It's alright, Jem. You are safe now. I have you," I say but I'm still far too angry to sound reassuring.

Jem just stares at me. I can feel the rapid rise and fall of his chest against my own. His body is going to take a minute to realize that the danger is over. He is safe now. I got there in time. Thank heavens. The thought that I might not have, makes my stomach heave.

My arms tighten as I hold him even closer, as if I need to reassure myself that he is really here. I really am holding him. He is mine to keep.

"H...how?" stammers Jem in a faint whisper.

"Colby called Barny," I explain.

"Oh," says Jem tonelessly, and he shifts uncomfortably in my arms.

I carry him over to my bed and gently lay him down, making sure to keep his pertinent parts covered with my jacket.

He looks up at me. His face is ashen and his bottom lip is trembling. "S...sorry," he rasps as his beautiful eyes fill with tears.

The physical pain in my chest is intense. It's crushing. Excruciating. I never knew emotions could feel like this. I throw myself down onto the bed and wrap my arms around Jem. He needs to understand.

"You have nothing to be sorry for!" I exclaim earnestly. "Telling the Council is what you are supposed to do. You were just following orders."

Jem just continues to stare at me. He looks completely shell-shocked.

"You're not angry?" he says tentatively.

Crushing my heart even more. I yearn to punch everyone who has ever made him feel this way. All the people in his life who were blind to his dazzling brilliance and failed to acknowledge it.

I shake my head, "Not at you."

I hope my sincerity is clear. I'm trying to let my possessive rage drain away. The very last thing I want is for Jem to be scared of me.

Jem lets out a soft sigh and drops his gaze. I gently put my fingers under his chin and encourage him to look at me again. His beautiful eyes return to mine and I smile. His eyes are full of confusion and bewilderment but I can't see any fear.

"Never again, Jem. Never again. There is never going to be anyone else but me. Forever and always."

His eyes grow even larger and his mouth drops open. He stares at me. Then a flush spreads across his cheeks and he gives a slight shake of his head.

"You can't decide that," he whispers.

"I can," I say coldly. "I'm a prince and I get what I want, and what I want is you."

His brow furrows in confusion, and the sight breaks my heart. He shouldn't be confused that I want him.

"Why?" he asks in a completely bewildered tone.

"Because you are incredible Jem. You are kind, clever, fierce."

There is a look of complete disbelief on Jem's beautiful face. This is pointless. I can't convince Jem of his worth with a few words. He has had a lifetime of being taught the opposite. Teaching him how wonderful he is, is going to take years. Years of devotion and worship that I am very happy to give.

I take a deep breath. "All you need to understand is that I want you. I want you to be my vessel, so I'm going to make it happen."

Jem looks so utterly astonished it's almost amusing. He tries to speak, but it is clear the words are just not coming. It is a lot to take in. I have rather bombarded the poor man. And besides, he is absolutely brimming with magic. So much so, that even a normal, everyday conversation would probably be too much.

I place a finger on his lips, and he stills instantly. "We can talk about it later. Right now you are very ripe. May I empty you?"

Jem flushes and nods. A deep hunger flashing in his eyes. Hunger for me. The sight of it ignites something deep within me. A feral, primal need. I want to claim Jem. Take him. Body, mind, soul and magic. I need to make every part of him mine. I want him to cry out for me. I'm going to fill him with so much pleasure that he is completely undone. Then I'm going to put all his pieces back together and cherish him forever.

It's going to be glorious.

Chapter Nineteen

Jem

My body is too hot. I'm burning up from within. Will's lips on my neck are both cooling and soothing. His kisses are so soft and so tender, they leave a trail of passion in their wake. igniting my desire. My body is alight with lust. My mind is spinning, lost in chaos. I can't fully grasp that I'm here, in Will's bed and not that dank basement.

I absolutely can't fathom all that nonsense Will was spouting about making me his vessel. He must have just been overcome by emotion. It's fine. I won't mind at all when he retracts his declaration later. I'm just so very grateful to be here. I'm going to relish this moment and try not to sob in relief that it is going to be Will who empties me. I don't want anyone else. I've never wanted anyone else. Just him. Only him.

Will kisses his way down to my chest. The feel of his gentle lips upon my skin is divine. I wish I was brave enough to let him press his lips against my own. I imagine it would feel incredible and he is the perfect person to give my first kiss to. If only I was not such a coward.

Pleasure shoots through me, a bright dizzying arc. Will's tongue is lapping at my pierced nipple, twirling the piercing around and around. The noise that spills out of my throat is positively filthy and I don't even care. I don't feel any shame with Will. Only joy. With him, everything is right and good. Exactly how it should be, yet something I have never experienced before. This is Will's gift to me.

His fingers drift a dance across my body. They claim my free nipple and start toying with it. The sensation shoots like electricity through my flesh, pooling between my legs. Driving me wild with need. I'm twisting and writhing and utterly at his mercy. My cock is so hard it hurts. It is leaking and throbbing. My ass is clenching around the butt plug and it feels so good. This is bliss and he has only touched my nipples. When he turns his attention lower, I'm going to completely lose my mind.

Not that I'm in any hurry. I could exist in this perfect moment for all eternity. In Will's arms. Subject to his tender attention. His delicious manly smell filling my senses. His presence surrounding me, bathing me with its warm glow. I feel safe. Wanted. Seen. It is everything I never knew I needed, everything that was missing in my life, and I want to weep with relief and gratitude.

I can surrender to Will. I know, with absolute certainty he will catch me. He won't let me fall. I can let everything go. I can just be. Pain, anxiety, fear and doubt can all melt away. In his arms, I am no longer alone.

His gentle hand whispers over my cock. A gentle caress. I whimper and buck into his touch. My magic is roaring within me, demanding release, it can sense Will, but can't reach him. It's imprisoned by my skin and it is making it furious.

Will senses my urgency. There is no need for words between us. He knows all of me.

His fingers leave my cock and gently tug at my butt plug instead. The pressure on my rim is divine, but it is merely an echo of what I truly need. I need Will's cock inside me. I'm craving it with a hunger that is burning through me, leaving me trembling with its intensity.

I want to be filled. I need to be stretched. I wish to be one with Will, our bodies joined. So close together that not even a molecule separates us. Sharing lust, desire, breath and heartbeats.

He works the plug free and I whimper at the empty feeling. My hands claw at his shoulders, pulling him closer to me. Demanding him.

His cock pushes at my entrance, and I cry out in relief. My head tilts back, and he slides into me. Where he belongs. My legs wrap around his waist, my arms around his neck. I'm clinging onto him as if he is the only life buoy in a dark and stormy sea. And it's true. He is my light in the darkness. The one who can save me.

He starts to move and fireworks of joy explode in my mind. There is so much pleasure, so much satisfaction, I cannot contain it all. It's raging through me. Rearranging the very cells of my body and reforming me into someone new. Someone better.

He thrusts, and I rise up to meet him. I'm clawing at his back as I sob with overwhelming sensation. I'm being scattered. I'm falling apart. I'm nothing but euphoria and desire. Will is the only thing that exists. I can feel his magic and it is calling to my own. An enticing, irresistible siren song. I want to give it to him. All my magic, all my everything. Will can have all of me. I give it gladly.

I look up at him and the moment our eyes meet, I feel a jolt of something between us. Something intense and unfathomable. It feels almost like power and a lot like a connection. Something snapping into place and tying us together. Binding us.

His eyes are warm. Full of tenderness, as well as a little awe, as if he can't quite believe he is getting to make love to me. There is also dark desire swirling in his depths. A near feral lust. It makes my heart sing to see him look at me like that.

In this intimate moment. I can see all of him. The window to his soul is well and truly open. And he shines with light. He is a good man. To the very core.

I wonder what he is seeing in me? It's hard not to wince. But I manage it. I will not ruin this moment for anything.

He shifts his angle and I see stars. I'm making a high pitched keening noise and I can't stop. Pleasure is consuming me. There is nothing left but carnal delight.

Will rocks me again, his cock rubs over that exquisite spot inside me and I am undone. Waves of ecstasy wash over me, driving me to another plane of existence. It feels like heaven and nirvana. My body is clenching around Will, milking him. My cock is spurting its release. Every muscle I possess is trembling. I ride my peak long and hard as my magic pours out of me and finds its home in Will.

I wail and thrash until I'm utterly spent. I'm empty. I have surrendered every part of myself. Given my all. There is nothing left but peace, contentment and darkness. It is heavenly.

Chapter Twenty

Will

My phone rings. The tone is shrill and piercing in the silence of my room. Jem stirs and murmurs something sleepily, but doesn't wake. I grab the phone. I'd switch it off, if it was not that particular ringtone. The one I am not permitted to ignore.

"Hello, Mother," I say quietly as I tiptoe naked across the bedchamber. At the door to the sitting room, I turn and pause. Jem hasn't woken up after passing out when I emptied him. I know it happens sometimes and is perfectly normal. But I hate leaving him. Especially as he began the evening in that awful basement.

"Wilhelm, what is this business about you punching a lord over a vessel?"

I stifle my groan and reluctantly close the door. I need to deal with my mother, then I can return to Jem.

"He deserved it," I tell my mother. There is no point in asking her how she knows. The woman is omnipresent, it is as simple as that.

She doesn't reply but I can hear her disapproval. I put her on speaker, and place my phone on the cabinet so I can pour myself a drink. I need reinforcement when dealing with my mother at the best of times, and today is going to be a doozy. I'm imbued with Jem's marvelous magic, I feel more powerful than I have ever felt in my entire life. But it is still not enough to make me feel confident about facing my mother. I doubt anything in the universe can give me that power.

I take a deep breath and brace myself. I can only do my best. It won't be enough, but it is all I have to offer. The only thing I can do.

"I'll give Lord Smythe some hush money, don't worry about that Mother. I will deal with it."

She makes a slight huffing noise that voices all of her displeasure. I down my whiskey in one swift gulp, relishing the burn down my throat.

"I'm claiming the vessel as my own." I think my voice sounds steady, calm. I hope I sound confident and resolute.

Silence.

"His name is James Cambell, he is the brother of Duke Sothbridge."

My mother sighs. "I know he is disgraced, Wilhelm. Do you really think I don't know who you are spending the summer with?"

"He doesn't deserve to be disgraced!" I snap. "He was abused by his trainer, it wasn't his fault!"

I should have known that Mother would have a full report on Jem. She probably knows more about him than I do. It's a little disconcerting and a whole lot infuriating.

"I have every sympathy for the boy, but that doesn't change the facts. In the eyes of society, he is disgraced. He is not suitable to be your vessel, and besides, your vessel should be your future spouse and preferably a woman. You need heirs. Have you forgotten your station?"

I grit my teeth. "I haven't forgotten my station, nor the fact that I'm gay. A surrogate is a perfectly acceptable way to provide heirs, Mother."

The silence is deafening. I pour another whiskey. I know my mother's tactics, but waiting for her reply is still making me sweat.

"Please do not tell me you are under the illusion that you can marry him?"

I swallow painfully. I'm the worst kind of asshole because, no, I'm not thinking I can marry Jem. Even though he deserves no less. I love him, but I'm too frightened of the consequences. I'm too much of a coward to put him first and fuck everyone else.

"Good," says my mother, even though I haven't said a word. "Bring him home to Bavaria if you must, but you will keep him discreetly."

"Yes, Mother," I say weakly.

She is being far more reasonable than I expected. But the thought of treating Jem as my dirty little secret is leaving a sour taste in my mouth. Is it really the best I can offer him?

The phone goes dead as she does her normal habit of hanging up without saying goodbye. I let out a shaky sigh of relief and try to release the tension from my shoulders. It's over. I've talked to my mother, now I can return to Jem.

I hurry back to my bedchamber. The bed is empty, nothing but a tangle of sheets. My heart pounds frantically in my chest. Jem must have slipped through the connecting door to his rooms. I hate that he woke up alone.

I chase after him. His bedchamber is empty, the bed neatly made. Panic itches along my skin, then I hear it.

The shower. Jem is in the shower. My feet stop outside the bathroom door. I can't exactly barge in and demand to know if he is okay.

Tentatively, I try the door handle. It's locked. Allright, the poor man obviously needs some privacy and space. I can give him that. I'll go down to breakfast so that it doesn't seem as if I'm stalking him. Then I can check up on him later. It's a very sensible plan.

After a very brief wash and throwing on some clothes, I head down to the breakfast room.

Barny looks up from his toast. "How is Jem?"

"Fine," I say with a smile.

I hope I'm not lying. Barny nods and turns his attention back to his breakfast. He is being very polite and not prying for more information, even though the drama of Colby's phone call, and my dashing off in a rage, must be swelling him with curiosity. He is a good lad.

I take a closer look at him. He looks pale. Guilt washes over me. I'm supposed to be here to look out for him. Something I have failed most spectacularly at. And now I'm ignoring him to chase after Jem. I'm a terrible uncle.

"How are you?" I ask.

He gives me a weak smile. "I'm fine, thank you. My social calendar is filling up nicely. I was wondering if you would attend some events with me?"

"Of course!" I say brightly as I pour myself a coffee.

Accompanying Barny to balls and dinner parties is exactly the type of thing I'm supposed to be doing. The entire reason for my stay. But the thought of it is making me feel sick. I can't exactly bring Jem. I suppose I could try to pass him off as Barny's chaperone, but I suspect that wouldn't work either. Chaperones are supposed to increase respectability, not lower it.

However, leaving Jem here alone while I swan off to glittering social events, feels all kinds of wrong. But what can I do? Rightly or wrongly, he is disgraced. My mother is correct in that regard.

No host is going to want him at their event. I could ignore all of that, and bring him as my plus one. Nobody would dare say anything to my face. But that will make no one happy. Least of all Jem. Being stared at and whispered about, doesn't sound like fun at all.

A faint clinking sound catches my attention. Barny's spoon is rattling against the edge of his cup as he stirs his tea. Is he alright? Why is he shaking? Concern flares through me.

"Perhaps sir should return to his bedchamber," suggests Jeeves.

Barny drops his spoon and flushes a bright red. "Umm...er...Yes, that is a splendid idea. Please excuse me, Uncle Will."

I nod absentmindedly. Barny clambers to his feet, turns sharply on his heels and shuffles away with Jeeves stalking behind him like a dark shadow. It's hard to believe what I am witnessing. My nephew is walking off to his rooms to be emptied by his butler. How has it come to this?

Though, I have to admit that the spell casting is exquisite. I've only figured out what is going on by logic. I can't sense a thing about Barny's magic, but the situation is still so very precarious. It could all come crashing down at any moment. No spell is infallible. Barny really does need to be wed as soon as possible. And without causing any drama or arousing any suspicion.

Which means I have to leave Jem behind. I can't risk the attention that bringing him will cause. Barny is my nephew, I owe him a duty of care. Especially since if I had been watching him properly, like I should have been doing, instead of fondling Jem on the balcony, he never would have been tapped in the first place.

But, how on earth I'm I going to convince Jem that he is worthy, and that I'm not ashamed of him, when I cannot invite him to accompany me?

Despondently I reach for a crumpet. Why does life have to be so difficult? Jem is wonderful. A sheer delight. He makes me happier than I have ever been. Loving him should not be so hard. It's in times like this that I wish I was a mundane, with no title. I'd be poor, but I'd be free.

And freedom, especially when it comes to love, is priceless.

Chapter Twenty-One

Jem

Why am I crying? Will rescued me from my terrible decision and by some miracle he doesn't hate me. I've just had the most incredible sex of my entire life. I'm no longer bursting with uncomfortable magic. Everything is wonderful.

So why am I in the shower sobbing like a baby? Crying like I haven't since I was a small child. Why did I wake up in Will's bed and then feel so strange? So empty, and not just in a magic way?

I'm clearly losing my mind. There is no other rational explanation and nothing else makes sense.

This water is scalding, but I'm shivering. I have one hand pressed against the tiles and I'm leaning heavily, but I don't think it is enough to save me. Any minute now, I'm sure I'm going to slide to the floor.

The water swirls and whirls around and down the drain. The spray sounds like rain and the noise echoes through me. The sights and sounds consume me. By some miracle I haven't collapsed into a weak heap on the floor of the shower. I can't pull myself together, but the tears have stopped. There are none left. I'm hollow and numb.

Some part of me turns the shower off. My body goes through the motion of rubbing a towel over my wet skin. Drying my hair is too insurmountable a task, so I don't even attempt it. Instead, I stagger to my bedchamber. Struggling into some sweatpants and my large comfy hoodie is exhausting.

Now all I can do is sit here on my bed with my head bowed while water steadily drips from my hair onto the floor.

"Jem?"

I blink. I have a feeling that wasn't the first time someone said my name. I look up. Will is walking towards me. His eyes widen.

"Oh, my precious, it's okay, I'm here now. I've got you."

Suddenly Will is manhandling me and before I know what is happening, I'm lying on my side on the bed and Will is curled around my back, one strong arm encircling my waist. It feels wonderful. My body sags against him, releasing tension I didn't realize I was holding. A dry sob flows out of me, I'd think I'd cry if I wasn't all out of tears.

"It's okay, Precious. Everything is okay," rumbles Will behind me and he kisses the top of my head even though my hair is wet.

"I don't know what is wrong with me," I say as my breath hitches uncontrollably.

Will tightens his grip on me and pulls me even closer. "Being emptied can be really intense, it can cause something like a sub drop. Never mind all the stress of being in that basement."

What? My mind feels as if it is wading through treacle. Although, I don't think that's the sole problem. I think Will is talking about something that I have no knowledge of. I despise feeling uneducated. It makes me squirm.

"I have no idea what a sub drop is," I confess.

He kisses my head again. "That's okay Precious, I'll tell you all about it later. Right now, all you need to know is that I'm very sorry that I left you to wake up alone. I should have been there to hold you."

I still don't understand what he is talking about. Waking up alone is perfectly normal. It's what adults do. I certainly have never woken up any other way.

And I've been emptied countless times before and never felt like this. Though, thinking about it, I've never been emptied so thoroughly before. I remember hearing something about how the more a vessel enjoys themselves, the more of their magic their body surrenders.

It seems like Will is right. Which is not surprising. But I'm struggling to accept that I needed a hug. I'm not a touchy feely sort of person.

"I don't need to be held, I'm not a baby. And what's with all this Precious stuff?"

Will chuckles. "It's what I'm calling you from now on. My Precious Jem."

It's the most stupidest thing I've ever heard, yet my heart is fluttering and my stomach is swooping. My very soul is singing with glee. I have an intense urge to preen. It's embarrassing as hell. I've never been a soppy person, it seems silly to start now.

"You sound like Gollum," I grumble. It is the only defense I can come up with.

Will laughs, a deep laugh. It rumbles through me. His chest moves along my back as his lungs rise and fall with merriment. It feels nice. I could lie here in his arms forever, listening to his happiness.

I wriggle closer, until there is not the slightest space between us, and close my eyes. My heartbeat is settling. My breathing feels easier. It seems my body responds to Will, and not just in a lustful way. I swear it should feel alarming, but it feels the very opposite. This man is astonishing.

"Okay," he says while still laughing. "I'll be your Gollum and you'll be my Precious Jem."

"That is the cheesiest thing I have ever heard," I say while shaking my head ruefully.

"So," says Will and I can feel his shrug against my shoulders. "It's not like the cheese police are going to come and arrest us."

I groan. He is too young for dad jokes but he is definitely headed that way. He is going to be absolutely cringe worthy when he is older. I hope I get to see it.

"Are pet names a claimed vessel thing?" I hear myself say, and I wince.

Why must I pick at things like a scab? Why do I prefer to make myself bleed rather than leave things alone? I could have just enjoyed this moment for a little longer. There was absolutely no need to goad Will into admitting that he isn't going to claim me. Words spilled during sex mean nothing at all.

His head moves down, and he kisses my shoulder. "I think it is an us thing."

That does not answer a thing. He doesn't seem awkward or resentful. He seems perfectly calm. What does it mean?

Is he really going to claim me, make me his and keep me? Or has he forgotten that he ever even uttered those words?

"Am I a claimed vessel?" I ask, and I hate how small my voice is. But at least somehow I was brave enough to ask.

He says nothing and my heart sinks. I was stupid to dare to hope. What was I thinking? I know better than that.

Will's arm disappears from my waist and he moves away from me, but just as cold horror and dismay starts to rush into me, he gently turns me over to face him. His arm wraps around my back and he pulls me close again. Envelopes me with his warmth. I stare helplessly into his kind brown eyes. He smiles at me.

"Yes, Jem," he says intently. "You are mine."

Chapter Twenty-Two

Will

Jem looks divine on horseback. I don't know why I'm surprised, he is the most beautiful man I have ever laid eyes on, so of course he looks damn good. He'd look stunning, anywhere, anytime.

Though I swear the sight of those tight cream jodhpurs clinging to his shapely thighs is especially appealing. His seat is perfect. Jem is an excellent horseman, and watching his hips roll as he moves effortlessly as one with the horse, really, really makes me wish it was me he was riding.

He looks over at me and smiles, aquamarine eyes sparkling. It's just a leisurely ride around Barny's estate but he looks so happy that I almost feel bad for being so consumed with horny thoughts. Almost.

I'm not a complete monster, and my heart is singing with joy to see him so fully recovered from his drop. He is a resilient man. The thought wakes a dark voice within me.

Jem is as tough as old boots because he has had to be, for his entire life. I frown and purposefully pack my sour thoughts away. Not today. Today is blue skies and spending time with Jem. A good and happy day where all feels right with the world.

Tomorrow is soon enough for dark clouds and worries.

"It's a beautiful estate," says Jem, and he sounds sincere. He is not just making polite small talk.

The grounds are lovely, he is quite right. It's all lush green grass and rolling hills in the distance. But I'm not paying our surroundings any heed at all.

"I agree, the view is very beautiful," I smirk whilst very obviously giving him a lecherous once over.

He rolls his eyes at me, but he smiles, and that is the only thing that matters. It feels as if it is the only thing that matters in the whole wide world. Jem's smiles are precious.

"Are you and Barny going to attend Duke Humberland's ball on the weekend?" asks Jem.

I wince and shamefully drop my gaze. So much for dark clouds being for tomorrow.

Jem sighs. "Will, I'm not a drama queen. I know I'm not invited. It's not your fault."

Hope flutters in my chest, but surely it can't be as easy as this? "You're not upset?" I ask tentatively.

"I've been disgraced my whole adult life. I'm used to it," he says with a shrug.

I don't know what to think about this. On one hand, I'm happy that he is so calm and accepting, on the other hand, I'm furious that this is his reaction. He shouldn't be so resigned to the injustice of it. I know it is not a lack of spirit on his part, more that it has been beaten into him, and even worse than that, part of him believes the lies that have been told.

"It's not fair!" I spit vehemently.

Jem fixes me with a stern stare. "Whatever made you think life was fair?"

I swallow. He is right. I know life isn't easy for most people, but I was born a prince. I've worn privilege my entire life. It's hard to remember that doors open more easily for me than they do to others, and this is the first real obstacle I've ever faced. I'm used to having the power to get what I want.

"Last one to the tree line is a loser!" calls Jem.

Then he is gone and I'm staring at the roan rear end of his rapidly disappearing horse. The little shit is distracting me on purpose and I don't mind at all. I grin and urge my horse into a gallop. This is the life. Wind in my hair. Thundering hooves beneath me. Jem just up ahead where I'm going to catch him in a minute.

I gain good ground. The trees are just up ahead and I can overtake him easily. He is a fantastic rider, but my horse is bigger and faster than his. I guide my steed right up to his and then, with the help of some magic, I pluck Jem off of his horse and place him in front of me.

Jem squeaks in indignation and surprise, but settles into my saddle beautifully. His abandoned horse snorts its displeasure, but follows along behind us nicely. I slow my horse to walk and we almost serenely enter the shade of the trees.

"You cheated!" breathes Jem.

"I never claimed to be honest" I say as I nuzzle his neck.

Jem leans back against me. Surrendering to my embrace. His thighs are pressed against my own as our legs follow the same curve. I let go of my reins. The horse shakes its head but continues walking gracefully. It clearly knows this path around the estate well. My hands unbutton Jem's Jodhpurs, undo the fly and pull his cock out into the summer air.

"What are you doing?" he gasps.

"Well, since you are sitting in front of me, technically you won, so I'm giving you your prize."

I give him a long, snug stroke. He groans and his head drops back to rest on my shoulder. Satisfaction coils through me. I continue to play with Jem's cock and it rapidly fills and hardens in my hand. I roll his barbell piercing and he moans.

"This is debauched!" he says.

"Does that mean you want me to stop?"

"Not at all."

I'm grinning so much my face is hurting. This moment is wonderful. It's cool in the dappled shade of the trees. The gentle sway of the horse is comforting. Jem's lithe body leaning against me is heavenly and the feel of his cock throbbing in my hand is utter bliss.

"What's the poor groom going to think when your horse comes back with jizz in its mane?"

My laugh spills out of me. Free, joyous and unrestrained. Jem is such a delight.

"What makes you think I'm going to let you cum?" I tease. "Maybe I'm going to toy with you and edge you until we return to the stable. Then you'll have to hide your hard-on from the groom. Which in these very tight jodhpurs is going to be tricky."

"Will!"

The way Jem says my name is electrifying. It's part complaint, part pleading, and all parts hunger and need. My cock throbs in response and I quicken the strokes I am giving him. His breath hitches and then he lets out a low keening noise.

Maybe I will let him cum. The sounds he will make will be music to my ears. The thought of him writhing and helpless in my arms, lost to his pleasure, is wonderful.

I flick his piercing and he whimpers beautifully. He deserves all the pleasure I can give him. He has been far too neglected in his life. Though, some dark, insidious part of myself takes delight in that. I'd be consumed with jealousy if there had been others of significance in Jem's past. The knowledge that I am the first to show him true pleasure, sets my soul alight with a dark, possessive glee.

Jem is mine.

His hips start to grind against me, and the pressure and friction on my imprisoned cock is intense. It forces a grunt out of me.

Then Jem thrusts into my hand. I place my free hand on his hip and still him with some gentle pressure. He will take what I give him, no more and no less. He whimpers, but obeys my wordless command. I grin and tighten my grip on his cock in reward. He shudders in my arms. I love him like this, all compliant and surrendered. I love him in all his different moods, but this one sets my soul on fire. I have never felt the level of gratification that I am feeling in this moment.

I quicken my pace, tugging on his perfect cock in earnest now. It is hot and swollen. Throbbing and pulsing in my hand. Beads of pre-cum leaking from the tip. Jem rests his hands on my thighs and his touch burns into me. Soft carnal noises of joy are spilling endlessly from his lips.

I want to see him peak. I turn my head and my lips find the shell of his ear. I kiss it. I nibble it. I run my tongue along it, and he erupts. His body is pressed so close to mine that I can feel how his muscles tense all over his body. The breathless, strangled sound that comes out of his throat sinks into me. His cock jerks and his cum spurts out, falling onto my hand, but I don't stop. I keep pumping. Keep milking. I want him to give me every last drop.

Faint shadows of his luminescent magic seep into me. I emptied him recently, so it's only enough to make me shiver, but it is still a euphoric sensation.

He wails and I can tell that oversensitivity is causing him to dance that line between pleasure and pain. I keep going. He sobs and it is starting to sound more like discomfort than joy, so I release him.

He sucks in a long shuddering breath and collapses boneless and utterly spent in my arms. This is glorious. I nuzzle the top of his head tenderly.

I never knew horse riding could be so much fun.

Chapter Twenty-Three

Jem

Lying in bed curled up with my Kindle, is the best way to spend an evening. I don't need to go to a stupid ball. I'd probably hate it anyway. For all sorts of reasons. Including the fact that I'd be bound to run into mages that I've been sent to when ripe, which would be all kinds of awkward and uncomfortable. Never mind all the other people who would give me snooty looks.

While imagining Will flying into a fit over it, and putting them in their place, is a delicious fantasy, the reality would be grim. So this is fine. More than fine. Especially since Will is going to be feeling guilty, so I suspect that the moment he is home, he is going to race up here to my bed and make it up to me.

It's an evil thought. Will has nothing to feel guilty about. He did not create my situation. But I'm only human, and very willing to reap the rewards.

Someone coughs softly in the doorway of my room and I jump out of my skin. The man is wearing a dark suit.

He is not especially tall, or especially anything. The word nondescript could have been invented for him.

Unease trickles down my spine and my stomach lurches. I'm fairly certain that I've met all of Barny's staff, yet I swear I have never seen this man before. Even aside from that unsettling fact, the stranger just oozes menace. Something is definitely wrong and my primal instincts are screaming danger at me. It feels as if my life is in peril.

I stare at him warily and pray I'm just being paranoid. He glides across the room, to the writing desk and pulls out a blank piece of paper and a pen. He sets them neatly on the writing surface.

"Write Prince Wilhelm a letter explaining why you are leaving him," he says in a soft voice.

Shit. My instincts were right. This isn't good at all. I try to swallow but my muscles have forgotten how to coordinate. Of course Will's family aren't going to be happy about me. Now that it has happened, it seems blindingly obvious that this was the inevitable outcome. I should have seen it coming. Will should have seen it coming. We are both a pair of idiots.

I fix the stranger with my best stubborn stare. How good is the Bavarian Secret Service anyway? I'm assuming that is what he is. He seems far too professional to be an amateur. He meets my gaze evenly and his eyes are cold and emotionless. Ruthless. I shiver.

"I see you are one of those," he says so softly that I have to strain to hear him.

"One of what?" I ask. I can't help myself.

"A stubborn one," he answers tonelessly. "It just means I have to threaten Harry and Colby. It would be such a shame if they were to get into a car crash."

THE PRINCE'S VESSEL

Adrenaline and terror runs through me. I'm trembling and I can't breathe. Dizziness is taking my sight. The bastard. I bet he knows that is how my parents died and he has guessed that it is a personal fear of mine. That I'm going to lose more people that way. Just one day gone. No warning. No ability to do anything about it. Just one day they are here and the next they are not.

I flounder out of bed and stagger over to the writing desk. The blank paper glares at me.

"Make it good," says the man. "Make it so he doesn't come after you or try to call you. If he does, I'll know you failed."

I've never hated anyone so much. Fuck this guy. Fuck my life. What on earth am I going to do? Tears of frustration well in my eyes and I blink them away furiously. There is no way I'm going to let this asshole see me cry.

I take a seat and start to write. I'm hyper aware of the creep looming over my shoulder. There must be a secret message I can put in this note, some way to let Will know what is really going on? I can't bear the thought of him thinking I've dumped him and run away in the night.

I'm racking my brains but I can think of nothing. It's shocking to realize that we have not known each other for long. There simply hasn't been enough time to build shared moments and memories, and therefore shared references that only each other would understand.

It's a bitter truth and I hate it. Mostly because it feels so wrong. Surely I have known Will forever? My life is definitely defined by two distinct segments. Before Will and after Will. He means the world to me.

It can't all come crashing down like this. I can't just vanish. This is too much. Ten minutes ago, my life was perfect and now I am losing everything. The only man I will ever love.

I finish the letter without coming up with a way to leave any clues. Perhaps if I had more time, perhaps if I wasn't panicking and my heart breaking. But there is no time and my heart is shattered.

I sign the letter James instead of Jem, but that will not be enough.

"Good," says the dangerous man. "Now pack up your stuff, there is a car waiting to take you home."

Wordlessly, I obey. My body mechanically goes through the motions of gathering my things, while my mind free falls.

Home? I suck in a shaky breath, a tentative ray of hope. If they are just going to let me go home, it might not be the end of the world. It buys me some time at least. Some time to figure out how to communicate to Will safely.

It's far better than being locked in some basement somewhere. Or murdered. I shudder as my blood turns cold. There is no guarantee that those things are not going to happen. Just because he said I was being taken home, doesn't mean I'm going to make it there.

From Will's perspective, I'll just vanish into the night, never to be seen again. Just like I tried to make happen the night we met.

A fresh wave of adrenaline courses through me, as one ludicrous, insane idea pops into my head. But it is better than nothing.

I'm flinging my things into bags willy-nilly. The creepy guy is merely watching me with a bored expression on his face.

"I've left some things in the prince's room," I say.

He gestures at me to go through the connecting door. My heart is thundering. It picks up pace as it becomes clear that he is not following me.

This might work. My crazy plan has a chance. A paper thin one, but it is something at least. It has to be. Because it is the only thing I have.

Chapter Twenty-Four

Will

My hands are trembling so much that I can no longer read the words before me. Not that it matters. Jem's letter is seared into my memory, burned into my soul. I will remember every last word until the day I die.

He wants to go back to his old life. He relishes his freedom. He likes belonging to no one.

Jem is grateful for the time we spent together, and thankful for the happy memories. It was an enjoyable fling, and he wishes me all the best. But he does not want to see me again.

The horror of it is too much. This is going to break me. I'm going to break into a thousand pieces and never ever be the same again.

It is shocking how fleeting happiness is. How precious. Just a few hours ago my life was nearly perfect. Jem's disgraced status was the only dark cloud. Everything else was wonderful. I knew Jem hadn't fallen for me quite as hard as I had for him. But there was promise there. The seeds had been planted. I was sure of it.

However, if this letter is true, it was all in my head. Or rather, it is still all in my head, because I still believe it. Jem and I have something. Don't we? Or has everything I have been feeling been nothing more than a fantasy?

But how could it have never existed? Did I really just see what I wanted to see? Am I really so big-headed? I'm struggling to believe that. Jem is fond of me. I know he is. I can feel it in my bones.

Oh gods! My thoughts are chasing themselves in circles!

Jeeves discreetly lets me know that he has entered the room. I look up at him hopefully.

"It seems Mr. Cambell arranged for a driver to collect him. The staff report that he bid them farewell and left while appearing under no duress."

I stagger into a chair. "Are you sure? He signed it James, and he told me on the night we met that he is only ever called James when he is in trouble."

Jeeves's dark eyes glitter. "Indeed, Your Highness. I agree it warrants further investigation."

I'm staring at the butler, I know I am, but I can't stop. He is giving me hope. If he thinks this all seems suspicious, then it might actually be. His judgment is not impaired by wishful thinking.

If only Jeeves had been here and not at the ball in case Barny needed him. If only I had left my bodyguard here. But how was I supposed to know that Jem would not be safe when he was tucked up in bed?

"I should go to his house and talk to him," I say as I pull myself to my feet.

"I think that may be unwise, Your Highness."

Jeeves's words cause me to freeze. I was just deciding on whether to portal or drive to Jem, but now I'm staring at the butler in alarm.

"If Mr. Cambell was forced to leave under duress or threat, we do not know what danger is looming over him. Rushing in may cause a calamity, Your Highness."

I crumple back into the chair. Jeeves is right. I need to be careful about this. I can't just go barging in. Putting Jem in danger is the very last thing I want to do.

"So, what do we do?" I ask.

I'm a prince and I'm deferring to my nephew's butler, and I don't even care. Rank and station means nothing when it comes to the crunch. I've always known that. Seeing it in evidence is not surprising. If anything, it is a little reassuring.

"We research. Investigate. Reach out discreetly. Knowledge is power, Your Highness."

I nod my understanding and agreement. My mind is whirling through possible contacts, although I have a very distinct feeling that Jeeves is going to be far better at this than I am. I can well imagine that the butler has tendrils everywhere. Contacts all over. Probably even in the underworld.

"I cannot thank you enough for your help, Jeeves," I say with all the sincerity in my heart.

Jeeves bows his head. "You are very welcome, Your Highness. Mr. Cambell is a kind soul, he does not deserve the darkness of the world."

He truly does not, and it makes me happy that I'm not the only person who can see how brightly Jem shines.

Jeeves takes his leave, and the sudden loneliness is aching. I'd been so looking forward to reuniting with Jem.

The hours I'd spent at the ball had felt infinite. Now they are stretching out endlessly before me, with no clear indication of when I will get to see him again. Or any real certainty that I ever will.

The letter could be genuine. Or my foes could be greater than me. Any number of things could happen.

I rub at my chest but I don't think this crushing pain in my heart is physical. It's certainly not something a mere rub can ease. I have never felt so morose.

I should head to bed. A rest and a clear head is going to be far more helpful than sitting here brooding all night. But my limbs feel heavier than lead. My dark mood is growing, if it was not for Jeeves, I'd be utterly convinced that Jem really did leave me of his own free will.

But what if the butler is merely humoring me? Making me feel better. Stopping nobles from throwing hissy fits is part of his role. And he is excellent at his job.

Scowling, I drag myself to my bedchamber. I'll shower in the morning. Hopefully, I'll have some motivation then. Escaping into sleep seems so alluring. It is the only thing I can think of that could possibly ease my pain. Even if it is only going to be a temporary reprieve.

My clothes fall to the floor and I slip under the sheets naked. The bed is cold and empty. Too big for just one man. The linens have been changed. There is no trace of Jem's scent on the sheets. A heavy sigh escapes me.

My mind whirls. If Jem hasn't truly dumped me, then who would force him to leave? The only logical explanation is my parents. They have the most to gain from this situation. It's a low, but admittingly clever move. Pretend to be more or less accepting about my relationship with Jem. Then lean on Jem. In theory, I'd be none the wiser and assume it was just the natural course of things. Whereas, if they outright ordered me to leave him, I'd get my stubborn hackles up and dig my heels in.

They know me so well.

This is horrible. Either the man I love has up and left me in the middle of the night, or my parents are evil. Or some equally awful third option where insidious people are plotting against me for some as yet unknown nefarious reason.

Nothing about this is good.

I can't even get comfortable in this stupid bed. This pillow is very lumpy. I sit up and try to plump it up, but I feel something hard. Frowning in confusion, I lift the pillow up.

Jem's butt plug winks at me. The red fake ruby at its end glinting in the dim light. The plug he left behind after our first night together. The plug I returned to him and he hissed at me about it being a filthy version of Cinderella.

Now he has once again vanished in the night, leaving his prince a clue.

Jem wants me to come after him.

Chapter Twenty-Five

Jem

"Jem, have you been sat here all day?"

I blink up at Colby. I'd come into the sunroom just after breakfast. I'd brought my laptop and my coffee, with the plan of looking up the reading list for the master's degree, so I could get a head start.

But my laptop is unopened. My coffee looks cold, and judging by the sunlight streaming through the windows, it's past noon.

I blink again and try to get my bearings. Have I really been sitting here, staring into space and silently brooding all morning? It seems that I have.

Colby sighs and plonks himself down on one of the overstuffed sofas.

"If leaving your prince makes you so miserable, why did you do it?"

"He's not my prince," I mutter while seeing if my coffee is salvageable.

Colby pouts at me. I wish he'd leave me alone. I can't confess to him without putting his life in danger, and I just cannot pretend to be happy. I don't have it in me. If he keeps badgering me, I might let something slip. So it would be easier if he left.

Yet despite all of that, there is something soothing about his presence. It's nice to not be alone. And I do owe him a huge thanks. He got a message to Will and saved me from my stupidity the first time I left Will.

Colby probably thinks he needs to meddle once more and talk sense into me, but this time the decision is not mine. It's not self-sabotage, just plain old sabotage. And there is not a thing I can do about it.

"Have you chosen a surrogate yet?" I ask.

If I can steer the conversation onto a nice, safe topic, then I can have the best of both worlds. Colby's company, without the danger.

"We've made a short list but we are going to wait a couple of years," says Colby and I can see the conflict in his eyes. This is a subject dear to his heart and he'd love to talk more about it, but he is not daft and he knows I'm changing the subject on purpose.

I just know he is weighing up his options and trying to decide the best course of action. I can only pray he chooses humoring me and accepting my deflection, over diving in and grilling me. I'm not sure if I could survive the onslaught of a grilling by Colby. The man can be relentless.

"Would you like a fresh coffee, sir?" asks Tom as he pokes his head around the door.

"That would be lovely, Tom. Thank you," I say gratefully.

Coffee will be fantastic, and Tom's brief appearance has lessened the tension. Perfect timing, bless him.

However, Colby is still eyeing me a little suspiciously. Time to bring out my best innocent look. I put it on, and stare back at my brother-in-law. I can do this. He holds my gaze for a few heartbeats and then sighs heavily.

"I'm worried about you, Jem."

It's not a full retreat, but he is definitely wavering. I might be able to sway him and avoid a disastrous interrogation.

"I'm fine," I reassure with my best fake smile.

I'm the furthest from fine that I have ever been in my entire life. It feels like my heart is breaking, and I can't even tell a soul. If I mess up, people I love could be hurt. It's awful and I have never felt so powerless, so cornered, so much like a trapped animal. Bad guys could be watching me right now. Monitoring my every word, while I can't see or hear them. They could have placed a curse on me and the moment I breathe a word, terrible things could happen. It's enough to raise the hairs on the back of my neck.

"What are you going to do the next time you are ripe?" asks Colby.

My stomach heaves, and my blood runs cold. I can't even bear the thought of it, so I bury it deep, deep inside me, to deal with another day. It's not the healthiest of coping mechanisms, but it is the only one I have.

"Same as I always do," I say, with a shrug, but my voice betrays me and sounds strained.

Colby's eyes fill with pity. The sight makes me wince and I look away. I don't need anyone feeling sorry for me.

"Jem…I…er, never mind," babbles Colby and something in his tone pulls my attention back to him.

He doesn't sound like he is struggling to say something pitying. He looks like he is really desperate to tell me something, but he can't. That's interesting. Seems he has secrets of his own. I trust him, explicitly. He risked everything to save Harry's life. So, I have nothing to fear from his secrets and he is entitled to them. But that doesn't stop me from being curious.

He flushes and looks away. The silence stretches. I guess I'm not finding out, at least not today. But this still might be a good thing. If he is caught up in his own secrets, he might be distracted enough to not try to unravel mine.

I will be able to keep him and Harry safe.

"Can you show me your shortlist of surrogates?" I say.

The look of sheer relief on Colby's face is almost comical. The young man really is a sweetheart. This distraction will be good for both of us. I have the rest of my life to brood and mope. I should seize whatever little islands of reprieve pop up. It will be good for my sanity, what's left of it anyway.

Colby bounces onto the sofa I'm sitting on before shuffling up right next to me. He pulls out his phone and starts opening his photo album, just as Tom walks in with a fresh, steaming cup of coffee and a plate of biscuits.

I take a deep breath. I can do this. I have to do this. Letting people get hurt because of me is no option at all.

I'll miss Will forever and losing him hurts like hell.

But I'm used to pain.

Chapter Twenty-Six

Will

Using a portal is perhaps a little excessive, but frankly I am beyond caring. And besides, I still have so much of Jem's wonderful magic flowing within me, that I can easily spare enough.

I set the portal to form in my rooms in the palace. Being impulsive is one thing, wasting magic to appear somewhere I'm not as familiar with, is quite another. I'm still capable of rational thought, just about.

Homesickness washes over me the moment I step through. I'm such a homebody, it's ridiculous. But there is no time to be wistful now. I have things to do. I'll be returning home permanently in a couple of months, and I'm determined to do so with Jem by my side.

With that thought firmly in the forefront of my mind, I set off in search of my parents. At this time of day, they are likely to be eating in their private dining room.

Confronting them during dinner is a low move, but unsettling them and taking them by surprise is one of the very few tools I have at my disposal. And if they truly are to blame for forcing Jem to leave, then they deserve all my rudeness and much more than that.

I burst through the door, and the sight of my mother flinching fills me with guilt. As does the look of worry and concern that flows across her and my fathers face the moment they recognize me.

"Wilhelm? My goodness! Are you alright? Has something happened?"

My father says nothing, but the fact that he is stroking his white beard, is a sign that he is deeply concerned.

I swallow. Suddenly I'm not as confident as I was a moment ago. Doubts are starting to fill my mind. Perhaps my parents are innocent. Or perhaps I just want them to be because the pain of their betrayal is too biting.

"You had someone scare Jem away, that's what has happened, and now you are going to fix it."

My voice sounds confident, sure. As if I know without a shadow of a doubt what they have done. My parents have taught me well. Bluffing is a powerful tool. Acting as if I have uncovered their guilt, might very well cause them to confess.

My mother blinks innocently at me while I search her face for the lie. I can't see a thing, but that means nothing. I know full well what my mother is capable of.

"Oh sweetheart, has James left you? I'm sorry to hear that. Have a seat and I will pour you a drink."

Numbly, I obey her command and fall into a chair. She gestures at the young girl serving them to give me a drink. I should have known that my mother would not actually pour a drink with her own hands.

I take a sip of the annoyingly good white wine.

"Now tell us what has happened, dear."

She's humoring me. She's playing the part of a concerned parent. She is using terms of endearment for flip's sake. This is definitely suspicious.

I narrow my eyes. "What happened was, you decided you didn't like my vessel, despite never meeting him, so you arranged for him to be scared away."

My mother takes a sip of her wine. "I am sorry that James has left you, however he was not suitable for you and I will not pretend otherwise."

"He is the son and brother of a duke, how on earth is he not suitable?" I snap. Jem holds a rank that my parents would think was excellent marriage material for a prince.

My father coughs uncomfortably and my mother fixes me with her best stern look.

"You know very well why. You may be stubborn enough to think you can ignore it, but don't you dare pretend that you don't know. It is crass."

She looks away from me and sips her wine again. I'm trying my best not to let her get to me but I can feel myself deflating. My first plan of action is not working. My parents are not going to confess. It's time to change tactics. I take a deep, bracing breath.

"I have reasons to believe he did not leave of his own free will. So, if it wasn't you, it is a deeply alarming security risk. And if he did choose to leave, he is a vessel. And a disgraced one at that, as you so kindly pointed out, Mother. Him leaving without my permission is a huge insult to me and Bavaria."

Saying that last bit feels as if the words are burning my throat. I hate everything about it. But it is far too good a card not to play, and I need everything I have.

I pause. I definitely have their full and undivided attention now. And judging by the lines on my mother's forehead, she is stressed. Good.

"Therefore, I would appreciate a provision of resources so it can be investigated."

My father is staring at me with a very displeased look on his face. My mother's lips are pursed tight. They have no rational reason to refuse me and they know it. They are going to sit there stewing for a few moments while they desperately try to think of a way to deny me. Then they are going to have no choice but to surrender.

It shouldn't feel as good as it does. These are my parents. But I am a grown man and I'm going to be king one day, they can't hold my reins forever. They are going to have to release control. They are going to have to trust me to make my own decisions and deal with my own mistakes. Because, imagine the disaster if I become king and I've never done a thing on my own?

I sip my wine and wait for them to realize that I have them in a checkmate.

Eventually my mother lets out a pained sigh. "Very well, I will order the Secret Service to investigate."

"No, thank you Mother. Please arrange for an agent to report to me. I need manpower and specialist skills, but I want to lead the investigation."

For a moment it looks as if my father might actually say something. He opens his mouth to speak, but my mother shoots him a look and he picks up his drink instead.

"Very well, Wilhelm," says my mother with an air of great resignation, as if she is a great martyr. "Now, are you joining us for dinner?"

The food looks delicious, some pie with a flaky crust and creamy filling, with sides of asparagus and green cabbage.

"Yes, please," I say a little sheepishly.

Barging in here, accusing them of terrible things and then demanding other things from them, and then just sitting down to dinner as if nothing has happened, feels a little awkward. But we are a royal family, displaying a stiff upper lip and hiding our emotions is everyday life for us. It's nothing we can't handle. And it will be nice to spend some time with them in a calmer atmosphere.

I'll do my best to enjoy this dinner and then I am getting straight back to my mission. I will not rest until I succeed and I will not fail.

I'm going to get Jem back.

Chapter Twenty-Seven

Jem

The lights are blinding. A pulsing multitude of color. The music fills my ears. The bass reverberates throughout my entire body. I can feel the rhythm in my chest. It is still not enough to drown anything out.

I'm drunk. I'm dancing. I'm surrounded by strangers. And I'm brimming with magic, and all I want is Will.

My plan seems stupid now. Find a mundane with enough residual magic to empty me. Because at least he would want me and not my magic. It might be a vague echo of sex with Will. Or at least something easier to bear than submitting to a mage.

But no one here has any trace of magic. And they are devouring me with their eyes, bumping into me, their hands straying over my body, causing me to need to dance out of the way. None of them want me. They want my body, and I've discovered far too late that it's no better than only wanting my magic.

I should never have come, and now I can't remember how to leave. I'm so very drunk, so very ripe, my thoughts are scattered, tattered, things that I cannot keep a hold of.

I remember thinking that if I got drunk enough and ripe enough, that I would be able to tolerate giving myself to one of these men. How wrong was I. I still only want Will. The only man that I can't have. My sob is swallowed up whole by the noise on the dancefloor. No one knows my pain. It is mine to carry alone.

This is a disaster. By now, Harry and Colby will be looking for me. They've probably notified the mage council, so they can help find me before I detonate. I can't blame them for that.

I'm going to explode and die, or be arrested. I'm not sure which one is worse.

I should probably leave this nightclub before I kill any innocent people. But the thought drifts away before I can fully consider it. My body moves with the beat and my mind is nothing but lights and magic and the effects of too many cocktails.

Maybe I can drift away like this. Leave reality and all my problems far behind. Horror stories of vessels going insane, used to scare the shit out of me. Now it doesn't seem so bad at all. It might even be the best I can hope for. The only way out that is available to me.

Perhaps if I had not buried my head in the sand, and thought about how to solve this problem before it was upon me, I may have come up with something. But it is all too late now.

The facts are simple. I'm a vessel, I need sex with a magic wielder to be emptied. I can't face ever giving myself to anyone other than Will ever again. But I am disgraced, and he is a prince. He may not care about my status, but everyone else does. We cannot be together, and therefore I'm all out of options.

I really should leave. I don't want to hurt anyone when my magic explodes. Hopefully, my mind will crack first so I won't feel anything, but I need to leave right now, while I still can.

I look around. I'm surrounded by sweaty, dancing bodies. I can't see a route out. I'm trapped. There is no escape. Panic starts to bubble through me. I try pushing at a few people, but there is nowhere for them to go either. I'm in the epicenter of the dance floor. The crowd engulfing me is several bodies deep. And they are all too drunk, high or exuberant to understand that I'm desperate to escape.

The song, 'Murder on the Dance Floor,' starts to play disjointedly in my head and now I'm laughing hysterically.

A strong hand lands on my shoulder. Will's presence, magic and scent washes over me. No, it cannot be. I have to be mistaken. I have already lost my mind and I am imagining things. I'm bringing my wildest fantasy and longing to life.

My heart ratchets up to a thousand beats a minute. My body starts to shake with adrenaline. I whirl to face him and lose my balance. His hands catch both my shoulders this time, and he holds me steady.

My eyes aren't focusing, I can't see him properly, but I think he looks worried. He absolutely looks as handsome as ever. Even if he is all blurry.

"You can't be here!" I yell over the music.

Is he real? Am I hallucinating? If he is really here, then that is terrible news for Harry and Colby. I was ordered to stay away from Will, and now my brother and his husband are going to pay the price.

"Yes, I can!" says Will, or at least I think that is what he said. The music is damn loud.

He holds up his phone so I can see the screen. I peer at it. It takes a while for the words to stay still so I can read them. Then I have to read them several times, just to make sure.

It's an email. Will petitioned the council for use of a vessel for a spell casting he wanted to try. He stated a preference for me. The council have agreed. I'm assuming there is a similar message on my phone, which I've left at home.

I drag my eyes up to his face. Is this true? Will doesn't hate me for running away in the middle of the night? He figured out my clue? And he has found a way for us to be together? It will only work for tonight. It's a temporary fix, genius for its sheer simplicity.

I open my mouth to say something, but no words are coming. My magic surges within me, pushing for release. It can sense that a powerful mage is close. Dizziness washes over me. Will catches me. He picks me up into a bridal carry and I close my eyes and rest my head against his chest. It's Will. Somehow he is here and I'm in his arms, where I belong. It's not forever, but I will take it.

Dimly, I'm aware of the crowd parting before us, as Will strides out of the club with me in his arms. I couldn't care less what everyone must be thinking. Their thoughts are irrelevant.

The only thing that matters is that Will is here. He found me. He has saved me.

And now I get to spend one more night in his arms.

Chapter Twenty-Eight

Will

The dawn light is seeping around the curtains. Birds are singing noisily outside of the window. I haven't slept at all. I left Jem briefly, so I could have a quick wash and put my clothes back on, and since then, I've been lying here, holding him.

Now Jem is stirring. His beautiful eyes flutter open and immediately fix on me. They are far clearer and focused than they were last night. Relief washes over me.

"How are you feeling?" I ask.

He winces. "Like I really need a shower."

He sounds like his normal, delightful self. I chuckle, lean over, and plant a soft kiss on his forehead. He melts. There really is no better way to describe it. All the tight tension he was holding in his body surrenders to a gentle brush of my lips. It makes me long for the day when he lets me kiss him properly.

"How did you find me?" he asks in a quiet voice.

I shrug. "There are not that many gay clubs within walking distance of where you had the driver drop you off."

A beautiful flush colors his cheeks. It is a wonderful sight to behold. Somehow, it makes him look even more gorgeous, even though that should not be possible. He already is the most beautiful man in the whole wide world.

"Oh," he says. "I really would make a terrible spy."

I laugh and fight the urge to kiss him. His aquamarine eyes flash with warmth for a fleeting moment before filling with something far darker. His body goes rigid. My heart sinks. The sudden cold is painful.

"You can't be here," he whispers, as if he doesn't want to give voice to the words. Or perhaps that is just my wishful thinking.

I'm glad he is no longer out of it, and seems to be firmly back in reality. With no apparent ill effects from being so very dangerously ripe. But I despise that he is now remembering our situation. Last night, for long glorious hours, it didn't matter at all. We were just us, and everything else fell away.

I place my fingers on his chin and tilt his gaze up to meet mine. "Why can't I be here?"

He winces and tries to look away but I hold on firmly. "Because I don't want you to be."

He is quite convincing. He stares back at me resolutely and I start to waver. Doubts start to rush in. Is it really so hard to believe that Jem is a free spirit, who is simply not interested in me?

"Has someone threatened you? Placed you under a curse?" I plead.

Jem scowls deeply and anger flashes deep in his eyes. "If they had, I'd hardly be able to tell you, would I!"

I sigh and release him. He is right, of course. It was stupid of me to ask. I know the answer, he left his butt plug as a clue. I need to trust my heart. Trust the way Jem clung to me last night and cried my name. He wants to be with me. Leaving is not his choice. He can't confirm it with words, but I don't need them.

"I'm going to figure it out, Jem. I'm going to find whoever has cursed or threatened you, and I'm going to get you back."

Hope burns in his eyes and the sight of it fills me with joy, but then he snatches his gaze away and rolls over, turning his back to me.

"A prince who can't handle rejection, what a surprise," he says snidely.

His tone is biting, but I couldn't care less. I know what I saw in his eyes. I'm sure of it. He wants me, and that is all that matters.

Leaving his bed is the hardest thing I have ever done. Somehow, I find the strength to do it. He keeps his back to me and curls up into a small ball. His red dress is all wrinkled and disheveled, and his gorgeous hair is all over the place.

I lean over and plant another kiss on the top of his head.

"I will be back soon, my precious Jem, to formally make you my vessel. The whole world will know you are mine."

His shoulders stiffen, but he says nothing. I don't mind at all. I know he is not free to speak to me. I shouldn't torment him by lingering. Taunting him with my presence when he needs to watch his every word, is cruel. It's that knowledge, and that knowledge alone that gives me the strength to turn away and leave him all alone.

By the time I reach my car, I'm trembling. I really should take my leave of the duke and duke consort. They were kind enough to contact me when Jem went missing whilst ripe. But I just can't face it. I'm only human and I have my limits. I hope they can forgive me.

The driver pulls smoothly away and I feel a physical pain in my chest. Leaving Jem hurts so much. It is a pain like no other. I think I'll just sit here and stare blankly out of the window for a while. It honestly feels as if it is all I am capable of right now. I'm far too much of a mess to be able to do anything else.

Spending the night with Jem was bittersweet. It was wonderful, of course it was. But I don't want Jem for a mere night, I want him every night. I want to sleep with him in my arms. I want his smile to be the first thing I see every single morning. I knew this before. I knew it without a shadow of a doubt. And last night cemented the fact. Jem needs to be mine.

My thoughts start to darken and a heavy cloud settles over me. What if I can't fix this before the next time he is ripe? I doubt my little ploy of asking the council for him is going to work again. Either with the council or whoever is threatening Jem.

My fingers fumble with the top button of my shirt. Suddenly my clothes feel too tight and it feels as if I can't breathe. The thought of Jem being sent to someone else is unbearable. The images of him in that basement will haunt my nightmares forever. I promised him that it would never happen again. I promised that there would never be anyone else but me.

I don't make idle promises. I've never broken one. And I've never wanted to keep one more. I need to keep my promise to Jem, it is imperative. It is, unquestionably, the single most important promise of my entire life. But how am I going to do it? How am I going to solve this mystery and defeat the foes at the bottom of it, all before Jem is ripe again?

A groan escapes me, and I run my hands over my face and then through my hair. I never knew it was possible to feel this level of stress and anxiety. It is like living in a nightmare and I cannot wait for it to end. Waking up from this will be the most wonderful thing in the entire universe.

My phone buzzes in my pocket. Perhaps it will offer a distraction. I fish it out almost eagerly. It's Jeeves. My heart thuds. Has he found something? I have more faith in him than the secret agent I have been assigned.

"Good morning, Your Highness." His voice is calm and soothing, even over the phone.

"Good morning, Jeeves."

"It appears that Mr. Cambell's brother had a significant disagreement with the political faction he was previously a long-term member of."

That doesn't sound good at all. It is also extremely humbling. I had completely assumed that I was the center of the world and any plot against Jem was due to his association with me. I have jumped to assumptions, when in reality, it could be nothing to do with me, and all to do with his brother. Or even Jem himself. He could have pissed the wrong person off.

This is humbling as well as horrifying. If it is not about me, then the plot is going to be far more complex to untangle. We've been shoved back to square one. Further than that even, because now we need to go right back to basics and determine the motive.

The noise that comes out of me sounds like pure despair. This is awful. I don't want things to be worse than they were a mere moment ago.

"Shall I fill you in on the rest when you return, Your Highness?"

"Yes, thank you, Jeeves."

The butler is right. Phones and cars can be bugged. It is much safer to have this conversation in person, where I can protect us with a privacy spell.

Besides, waiting a few hours to hear even more bad news, sounds good to me. I'm not sure how much more my poor heart can take.

I bid farewell to Jeeves, shove my phone in my pocket and close my eyes. Tiredness washes over me. Perhaps I will be able to snooze. That sounds nice.

I might even get to dream of Jem.

Chapter Twenty-Nine

Jem

Part of me wishes to stay in this shower forever. Another part of me is worried about washing away the last lingering traces of Will's touch upon my skin. They might be the only thing of Will I have left and I want to cling to the echo of him for as long as I can.

I switch the shower off. Now I'm standing here in the cubicle, dripping. The sounds of draining water and my own ragged breathing are my only company. I have never felt more alone. There doesn't seem any point in moving. The only place to go is back to bed where I can stare at the ceiling and try to catch his scent in the sheets.

He found me. He saved me from being destroyed by my own magic. He rescued me from having to surrender my body to another. And now he is gone.

Last night was intoxicating. Passionate and exhilarating. It was perfect. And it should have lasted forever.

Why does fate have to be so fucking cruel. Why show me things beyond my wildest dreams and throw me into the arms of the most perfect man I could ever have imagined, only to take it all away?

What have I ever done to deserve to be taunted and tormented like this?

I drag in a great shuddering breath. Life is not fair. I know this. There is no point in whining about it. It's time to pull myself together.

I can't have Will and that is that. I should be grateful that I got to have one more unexpected night with him. A memory that I can now cherish forever.

My feet stumble out of the shower. My body is working on autopilot, which is just fine by me. I can't spool my thoughts in to concentrate on anything. I'm empty, hollow and drained, and not just in a magic sense. There is none of me left. It has all gone. It walked out of the door with the man of the dreams I never allowed myself to have.

I was single before I met Will. Now I am alone. And I'm going to be alone until the day I die.

A despondent sigh escapes my lips. Dreams, desires and longings that I have bottled up since I was a young teenager are escaping and running amok through my being. Once, a long time ago, I was a lot like Colby. All I had wanted was a husband, a home. A family. A simple and happy life.

Then in one night, I had lost it all. Now I have lost it all again.

Memories of Mr. Richards, sense my current weakness and seize the opportunity to invade me. I feel his hot breath on my ear. I hear him saying how I'm moaning so beautifully for him on the dildo that he can't resist giving me what I'm begging for. For him to take the dildo out and replace it with the real thing.

I feel his surprise at the moment I climax and my magic is freed for the first time and rushes into him.

He never planned to tap me, that much I'm sure of. He meant to withdraw and keep it all a secret. If I hadn't been so horny, no one would ever have known and my life would not have been ruined.

Familiar shame and guilt washes over me. I try to fight it. I call on Colby's words. 'If you stimulate someone's prostate enough, they will ejaculate. It's biology, not a character flaw.'

A deep, shuddery breath, and I'm able to shove all the dark thoughts and memories back down deep inside me, where they belong. I'm never going to let them escape again. They need to stay buried.

I sling a towel around my waist. Drying off seems like far too much effort. I shuffle to the door of the bathroom, open it, step into my bedchamber, and find myself face to face with the creepy man who ordered me to leave Will.

Terror erupts within me. My veins flood with adrenaline. My heart thuds. My muscles tremble in preparation for flight, but there is nowhere to go. I cannot escape. I swallow dryly and stare helplessly at him like the trapped animal that I am.

He should not be here. The house is well warded. Harry is a powerful and competent mage. No one uninvited should be able to get in.

"You were told to stay away from Prince Wilhelm," he says tonelessly.

"He requested me and snatched me from a nightclub, what the hell was I supposed to do?" I hear myself snap.

Oh, my gods. Do I have a death wish or something? Why on earth did I just say that? What is wrong with me? This is not the type of man to be confrontational with.

The creep seems completely unruffled. Not a flicker of emotion passes over his dead looking eyes. It is not the least bit reassuring.

"You should have written your letter so that his highness had no interest in ever seeking you out. As you were instructed to."

My heart rate increases. The promise is clear in his cold voice. He is here to make me pay for disobeying.

If I scream, will Harry hear me? Or will I merely be putting him in harm's way? This man is clearly dangerous, powerful and connected. He has threatened Harry, but in a sneaky, underhand way. Is he capable of taking Harry on face to face? Who would win in a duel? My brother is strong, this is his house, and he has Colby as his vessel. Can I risk it?

My thoughts scramble desperately in a freefall. I don't know what to do and my panic is building.

The creep steps towards me, and I instinctively step back, straight into the bathroom door. I don't remember shutting it.

Cold, dead eyes sweep over my nearly naked body, lingering on my pierced nipples. I shudder. I can't sense any lust from him and strangely, that just adds to my unease. I know how to handle lust. I know what to expect. This is uncharted territory and I'm floundering.

"I'm sorry," I try helplessly.

It seems worth a shot, but I doubt if an apology is going to be enough. It seems unlikely that forgiveness is in this man's wheelhouse.

He cocks his head. "I'm glad to hear it."

But he does not sound glad at all. He stares at me, and the silence and tension grows. My skin is crawling with it. It's a relief when he finally speaks again.

"However, I need to give you further encouragement to obey."

My heart is beating so loudly that I'm sure he can hear it. Summer light is streaming through the windows, but it is still dark in here.

He is peering into my soul, with a considering look on his face. I wait with bated breath to hear his judgment.

"Perhaps if something happened to Colby, you would understand what we are capable of."

I feel my eyes widen as cold horror consumes me. I open my mouth to beg, to plead, but I'm frozen. This is all my fault, not Colby's. Nobody else should pay for my mistakes, they are mine alone, and I am used to bearing the consequences.

A slow smirk spreads across his face. It makes him look truly evil, and it awakens a deep primal terror within me.

"I will go visit him now. I'm not usually interested in sex, but he does look so very submissive and breedable."

Something snaps inside me. As if my very soul cracks. I swear I heard it break. Suddenly all my fear is transmuted to white hot, all-consuming rage. I feel as if I am the very god of fury. I'm boiling with it. There is lava in my veins and violence in my heart.

The creep has a split second to widen his eyes before my fist slams into his jaw with a strength I did not know I possessed. I hear something crack. It sounds like bone. He staggers back from the force of it, arms cartwheeling. He falls. In slow motion, I watch as the back of his head slams into the ornate oak bedpost with a resounding crunch. His body jerks and is thrust out of its original trajectory, to fall slumped sideways on the floor.

Then everything falls silent and still. His intimidating presence has evaporated. He is nothing more than a motionless heap on the floor. I'm beyond numb. My eyes fix on the growing puddle of crimson under his head.

Suddenly, I can't breathe. I can't think. My numbness is consumed by a cacophony of emotions. Every part of me is screaming silently.

I'm not a murderer. I can't be a murderer. I never intended to kill anyone. Oh, my gods! What have I done! The horror and the weight of it all is crushing my lungs. I'm so dizzy that I cannot see.

My towel drops to the floor as I run to my bedside table. My hands scrabble at my phone. I have no idea what I'm doing until I hear Will's voice.

"Jem?" He sounds so hopeful as well as so concerned.

He is the one person in the world that I thought of. The person I trust the most. He will help me. He can fix this. I have absolute faith in him.

Some part of me is screaming that he is the very person I should not call. But that part of me is wrong. I can see that now, with absolute clarity. Will and I can face anything, if we do it together. I should never have doubted that. Staying by his side and dealing with the creep as a team, would have been the right thing to do. It seems so obvious. Why am I such a spectacular fuck up?

"I killed him!" I wail incoherently. Will won't know what the hell I am talking about. I need to string a coherent sentence together, but before I can even begin to try, Will replies to me.

"I'll be right there, Precious. Don't worry."

The phone goes dead, but I can feel a portal forming behind me. Sobs start to wrack my body. Will doesn't even care who I have killed. He is coming.

Everything is going to be okay.

Chapter Thirty

Will

The first thing I see when I step through the portal is that Jem is naked, and wet, and very upset. He throws himself into my arms and I hold him tightly. I quickly scan him for injuries and sigh in relief when I discover he is physically unhurt.

There is an abandoned towel on the floor by our feet, so I lift it to my hand with a bit of magic and wrap it around Jem without letting him go.

Then, and only then, do I allow my eyes to be drawn to the body on the floor. There is a faint flicker of life emanating from his crumpled form. Whoever he is, he isn't quite dead yet. But I have the distinct feeling that he does not deserve to be saved.

Duke Sothbridge bursts through the door and skids to a stop at the sight before him. I didn't even try to circumnavigate his wards when forming my portal. I wanted him to know I was here, and judging by the look on the duke's face, the man on the floor had been far more secretive in his arrival.

I watch as the duke takes in the sight of a body of a stranger on the floor, the puddle of blood, and his brother in nothing but a towel, trembling in my arms. Add in the fact that I left an hour ago by car, it has to be confusing.

"I'm sorry, I'm sorry!" sobs Jem.

He sounds hysterical. I pull him even closer to me, as if I can press reassurance into him. I hate that he is scared and upset. I loathe that I was not here for him when he needed me. Anger and dismay are fighting and coiling in my gut.

Duke Sothbridge stares at us. I feel for the poor man. I do not know if he suspected there was anything suspicious about Jem dumping me. This could all be quite a shock.

"I never meant to kill him!" Jem wails. "I just lost my temper and punched him because he was going to rape Colby to teach me a lesson!"

My eyes are on Sothbridge as Jem spills his words out. I see the duke pale, and then ignite with cold fury as he digests this information. I assume he realizes the same thing that I do. If this intruder was able to get into his house unnoticed, he would have been able to move freely within it.

It's midmorning, most married couples would not be in the same room at this time of day. The duke consort is probably alone right now. There is every likelihood that the threat could have been carried out.

"Your Grace, would you be so kind as to lower your wards so my people can come assist?"

Sothbridge blinks at me, with a slightly dazed look on his face, as if wrath is consuming all his thoughts, leaving no room for any other considerations. Then he nods and I feel the wave of his magic as he releases his wards.

Almost as soon as he has done so, the shadows in the corner of the room thicken. Then Jeeves steps through, with my secret service agent in tow. The agent looks a little green around the gills from the unorthodox mode of transport. But then his gaze falls to the man on the floor, and he turns an even deeper shade of green, as shock and recognition fly fleetingly across his face.

"Do you know him?" I snap.

The agent looks up at me in alarm. "No, Your Highness." His face is perfectly blank. If I hadn't caught him in his moment of disorientation from shadow walking, I never would have seen a thing.

I half carry, half drag Jem over to his brother and place him in the duke's arms. Then I spin on my heels, march over to the agent and throw him against the wall, holding him there by the lapels of his suit jacket.

"I am your prince!" I snarl at him. "One day, I will be your king. Do not lie to me!"

The man swallows convulsively. His eyes are wide and sweat drips down his face. He gulps audibly before clearly deciding where is safest to throw his allegiance.

"I'm sorry, Your Highness. Please forgive me. I do know him. That man is my superior. He reports directly to the king and queen."

His words hit me like a sucker punch to the gut. I feel breathless, winded. Hurt.

It was my own parents, after all. The very people who are supposed to love and protect me and want me to be happy. How fucking dare they! They think innocent people getting harmed is worth it to save their precious reputation? I am done with them, done.

I release the agent and let out a slew of swear words. Jeeves arches one perfect eyebrow at me.

"Just because I'm a prince, doesn't mean I don't know how to swear," I grumble.

"Evidently, Your Highness," agrees Jeeves smoothly.

I stride back across the room and reclaim Jem from his brother. I instantly feel so much better with his warm weight pressed against me. Then I draw in a deep breath.

"This vile piece of shit could possibly be saved, but I vote for letting him die."

I feel Jem jerk with surprise at my declaration as I scan the rest of the room. Sothbridge nods instantly and enthusiastically. Jeeves nods discreetly with the faintest of smiles stretching his lips. The agent fidgets for a brief moment before nodding his agreement. I grin in satisfaction.

"Jem, my precious. Do you understand? You didn't kill him, but we all think he should be left to die. Do you agree?"

I have to release my hold on Jem and push him away from me a little, so I can see his tear-filled eyes. He stares back at me, sniffs, and then nods. Good. It is all decided. I'd want the asshole to die for daring to scare Jem, let alone what he was planning to do to the duke consort.

I'm so very proud of Jem for knocking the bastard out and saving his brother-in-law. Trust Jem to be more protective of others than he is of himself. Undoubtedly because Jem believes he is not worthy of being saved. It breaks my heart that he thinks that way, and I truly hope that with time, I can get him to see what a special and spectacular person he is. And now I have all the time in the world to do so, because I am never, ever going to let anyone keep Jem from me ever again.

He is mine. My lover. My vessel. My precious Jem. Forever and always.

But there are some practicalities to deal with before we can celebrate our victory.

"Who knows the best way of getting rid of a body?" I say as I look at Jeeves.

"Without my husband knowing anything about any of this," adds Sothbridge, and I respect his desire to protect the man he loves. I agree that there is no need to give the sweet duke consort a reason to feel unsafe in his own home.

Jeeves inclines his head. "If I may be so bold, Your Highness and Your Grace. I have a suggestion."

I'm grinning so much my face is hurting. I knew it. My nephew really does have an excellent butler.

"I'm all ears, Jeeves," I say.

Everything is working out beautifully. I have Jem back. Jeeves knows how to get rid of bodies. The only thing left to do is put my parents in their place.

And with Jem by my side, I am invincible.

Chapter Thirty-One

Jem

My reflection stares back at me. I think I look respectable. I've tied my hair up in the neatest bun I can manage, but it is still clear I have long hair. Maybe I should cut it? It is not that unusual for vessels to have long hair, but looking more conventional can't hurt, surely?

But there is no time. We need to leave in a minute and hacking at my own hair with a pair of scissors is not going to produce very good results.

At least my dark suit is lovely. Hand made, professionally tailored. Nothing fancy, but it is definitely high quality. I still look like a twink, though. Nothing will ever make me look manly. Not that anyone wants a vessel that resembles a rugby player.

Oh gods, I've never been so nervous in my life. My thoughts are all over the place and utterly incoherent.

As if he can sense my distress, Will walks into my dressing room and straight over to me. He stands behind me and wraps his arms around my waist. Our eyes meet in the mirror.

"You look gorgeous," he says.

His words are just meant to comfort, but they still make my heart flutter and my stomach flip over. I don't know how he does it to me.

I huff out a sigh. "I'm terrified," I confess.

"Don't be." He shrugs.

I scowl at him. "Everyone gets nervous when meeting their boyfriend's parents for the first time! And yours are flipping royalty! Who tried to get rid of me, but I murdered the person they sent to do it!"

Will tightens his grip around my waist. My body sags back against him. His body heat seeps into me, and the feel of his strong, broad muscles is divine. I feel safe like this, protected. Cherished.

"I know, Precious. That's why we are doing this in a London restaurant, neutral territory. Hundreds of witnesses. It will be fine."

"They are going to hate me," I say, and it comes out as a hoarse whisper.

Anger flashes in Will's eyes. "So fucking what? We don't need their approval. You are my vessel and if they don't like that, they can shove it up their arse."

Laughter bubbles out of me. I can't stop it. It shakes my shoulders and puts tears in my eyes. Will gives me a puzzled look, one that doesn't help my mirth at all.

"Sorry," I say as I wipe a tear away. "It's so funny when you swear."

Will's eyes widen in surprise and then he chuckles as a warm grin spreads across his handsome face. He kisses the top of my head.

"Are you ready, Precious? It's time to go," he says gently.

A fresh wave of fear clenches at my guts, but I feel stronger now. It's not me doing this, it's me and Will. And I can do anything when his arms are around me.

I nod and we leave together.

The restaurant is all high vaulted ceilings and enormous chandeliers. Large windows look out onto the street and give a perfect view of the throng of press standing on the pavement.

Stepping out of the car and into a crowd of reporters had been quite an experience. One that Will had dealt with effortlessly and charmingly. He got us through and into the restaurant before I had a chance to catch my breath.

But there is no time to reflect upon the experience, as right now, the hostess is leading us over to Will's parents. The King and Queen of Bavaria.

I want to swallow but my throat is too tight. I'm sweating and I have a death grip on Will's hand. Far too soon and we are at the table.

"Your Majesties, I am pleased to present to you, Mr. James Cambell. My vessel," says Will.

My body remembers to bow to them both, and then I am being seated. I can't believe Will just declared it so calmly like that. I knew he was going to, it is kind of the whole point of us meeting like this, but I'm still shocked that he just jumped in so bluntly like that.

My gaze is fixed firmly on the perfectly white tablecloth, so I can't see his parents' reaction, but I can still sense a great deal of displeasure from them. This is awful. It is going to be the worst dinner of all time and I cannot wait for it to be over.

"How did the press find out that we were going to be here?" grumbles the queen.

"No idea," says Will cheerfully, and something in his tone makes me immediately suspicious.

"And what kind of restaurant does not have any tables away from prying eyes? It is so vulgar. Really, Wilhelm, you could have made a better choice."

"A little bit of press attention is always a good thing, Your Majesty," says Will calmly. "It reminds the people about how much they love royalty."

He is up to something. I just know he is, but I'm far too anxious to be able to spare any brain cells to try to puzzle it out. Besides, I trust Will. If I needed to know, I'd know.

The starter is served and I carefully lay out my starched linen napkin. Will and his parents are now making strained, polite small talk. The pianist playing in the corner is doing an excellent job of making her music unobtrusive. It drifts lazily along with the murmur of conversation and the clink of cutlery.

The starter is cleared away. One course down. Two more to go. No disasters so far. As long as I continue to remember my table manners, everything might be fine.

Oh, my goodness! Look at me sitting here demurely. Meek and quiet, not speaking unless spoken to. I'm acting like the perfect little vessel. Never knew I had it in me. Not that it is going to be enough to win his parents over. Nothing can achieve that. It can't undo the fact that I'm disgraced, and that is all they will ever care about.

Will's hand finds mine under the table and gives it a squeeze. He is right. Fuck them. I raise my head and Will grins at me. I look at his parents. They just look like old people. Not scary at all. I can do this.

"Excuse me," says Will as he gets to his feet.

Does he need the restroom? We are in a formal setting and he is a prince, so I politely get to my feet too. I may be disgraced, but I know my manners.

The rate of camera flashes coming from the window has increased dramatically. I really don't think a prince going to the toilet is that exciting.

Suddenly, Will is down on one knee in front of me. Did he drop his fork? Does he need to tie his shoelace? He really shouldn't be on the floor in public, he has an image to uphold.

Now he is holding a small navy blue box in front of him. He opens it and there is a beautiful gold ring inside, nestled on a bed of oyster colored satin.

"James Cambell, will you marry me?"

There are so many camera flashes, I can't see. People in the restaurant are gasping. The piano has stopped playing. My heart is thundering. I'm shaking. Will can't marry me, is he insane? I'm more than happy to just be his vessel. He doesn't need to marry me. I never dreamed in a million years that he would want to.

I glance over at his parents. They are smiling with joy and happiness. I blink. Oh, yes, of course. All the press are here. They can't exactly be glaring in pictures of their son's engagement. Will has played this very well.

Finally, I look at Will. He looks nervous. There is sweat beading his brow. His warm eyes are anxious but so full of love. I can see the truth shining out of him. He means this. He really does want to marry me, and it is not just a ploy to thwart his parents and firmly cement my place by his side.

Will wants me to be his husband as well as his vessel. He loves me. Will loves me.

I open my mouth, but all that comes out is a sob. I can't speak, so I nod frantically instead. Cheers and clapping fill the restaurant. Will slides the ring onto my finger with shaking hands. It fits perfectly.

He jumps to his feet with a huge dazzling grin on his face and I cannot stop myself. I launch into his arms and smash my lips against his own. I feel him stiffen in surprise and then he groans in pleasure. His arms encircle my back and the world falls away. I'm kissing Will. His lips are soft and gentle. His tongue slips into my mouth. I let him lead because I don't know what the hell I am doing, I've never kissed before.

The kiss deepens. Intensifies. It's passionate and all-consuming. It's igniting my desire and feeding my soul. The taste of him is intoxicating. Why on earth did I wait so long to kiss Will? This is incredible. I'll never be able to get enough. I want to kiss Will forever.

But he is pulling away. I whimper and try to chase after him. The sounds of the restaurant come rushing back. Oh shit. I can't devour Will in public. In front of his parents. Sheepishly, I let him go. My tongue traces the tingling sensation in my lips. Will's gaze drops to my mouth and heat flares in his eyes.

Then he looks up at me, and his eyes are burning with promise. 'Tonight,' they say. I nod and answer him with a look of my own.

'Tonight and every night. Forever and always.'

The Butler's Vessel

My head is spinning. My stomach hurts. I feel entirely too hot as well as too cold.

"Sir, may I suggest that you bend over the bed?"

Jeeves's calm voice cuts through the fog in my mind. My eyes fly open and find his dark gaze regarding me intently. I squirm. I'm standing half dressed in my bedchamber. My shirt is on but my trousers are in my hands. It's morning and I should be starting my day.

"No, I'm not ripe, I'm just unwell," I plead.

Jeeves does not release me from his stare. I whimper. My cock is hard. My body is remembering the feel of my butler's hands upon my hips, the slide of his huge cock inside me. I can't get addicted to him. This is just a temporary solution until I find a husband.

A terrible, wonderful, shameful and delightful solution.

"I'm fine," I insist, even though my magic is raging through me.

Jeeves arches one perfect brow. "I'm afraid I must insist, sir."

I whimper pathetically again, and I feel my cheeks heat.

"There is no need to be ashamed, sir," says Jeeves with kindness in his eyes, as well as a dark desire that makes my knees weak.

I don't think he is hating his new and unexpected duties.

Mutely, I discard the trousers I am holding and walk over to the bed. Taking a deep breath, I bend over it.

I don't hear Jeeves move, but I swear that man is part cat. I never hear him. I only know that he is behind me because he is pulling my underwear down to my knees.

I shove my fist in my mouth in a vain attempt to stay quiet. It's pointless. My butler is going to stuff me with his cock and I'm going to moan and scream. I'm going to be completely undone by ecstasy and pleasure while his soothing voice tells me how well I am doing, until I'm a sobbing, broken mess.

I can't wait.

Coming Soon!

Thank You

Thank you for reading my book, I hope you enjoyed it! If you haven't already found Colby & Harry's story, you can find it in Duke Sothbridge's Vessel

Want more Jem & Will?
How about a FREE exclusive bonus epilogue?

Tap the link to sign up to my monthly newsletter for instant access!

https://www.srodman.net/newsletter-sign-up.html

If you are already a subscriber, don't worry! The link was in the July 24th 2023 newsletter.
(If you signed up after that date, follow the link in your welcome email.)

Limited time offer **Not one, but TWO free books when you sign up!**

Sign up now and your welcome email will contain links not only for the bonus epilogue but also for a free copy of Incubus Broken and Omega Alone.

If none of that takes your fancy, how about exclusive short stories and opportunities to receive free copies of new books before they are released?

Sign up for my newsletter.

https://www.srodman.net/newsletter-sign-up.html

It comes out once a month, you can unsubscribe at any time and I never spam, because we all hate spam.

If the link is broken, please type www.srodman.net into your browser.
Or scan the QR code below.

Books By S. Rodman

For an up to date list, you can view my Amazon Author page HERE
Or view at www.srodman.net

Darkstar Pack

Evil Omega

Evilest Omega

Evil Overlord Omega

Duty & Magic: MM Modern Day Regency

Lord Garrington's Vessel

Earl Hathbury's Vessel

The Bodyguard's Vessel

Duke Sothbridge's Vessel

The Prince's Vessel

Found & Freed: The Unfettered

Unfettered Omega

Non Series

All Rail the King

Shipped: A Hollywood Gay Romance

Hunted By The Omega

DragonKin

DragonRider

Hell Broken

Past Life Lover

How to Romance an Incubus

Lost & Loved

Dark Mage Chained

Prison Mated

Incubus Broken

Omega Alone